ETHAN FROME

ETHAN FROME

◆

Edith Wharton

Introduction and Notes by
PAMELA KNIGHTS
University of Durham

WORDSWORTH CLASSICS

For my husband
ANTHONY JOHN RANSON
with love from your wife, the publisher.
Eternally grateful for your unconditional love.

Readers who are interested in other titles from
Wordsworth Editions are invited to visit our website at
www.wordsworth-editions.com

For our latest list and a full mail-order service, contact
Bibliophile Books, 5 Datapoint, South Crescent, London E16 4TL
TEL: +44 (0)20 7474 2474 FAX: +44 (0)20 7474 8589
ORDERS: orders@bibliophilebooks.com
WEBSITE: www.bibliophilebooks.com

This edition published 2000 by Wordsworth Editions Limited
8B East Street, Ware, Hertfordshire SG12 9HJ
Introduction and Notes added 2004

ISBN 978 1 84022 408 5

Wordsworth Editions
is the company founded in 1987 by
MICHAEL TRAYLER

Typeset in Great Britain by Antony Gray
Printed and bound by Clays Ltd, St Ives plc

GENERAL INTRODUCTION

Wordsworth Classics are inexpensive editions designed to appeal to the general reader and students. We commissioned teachers and specialists to write wide ranging, jargon-free introductions and to provide notes that would assist the understanding of our readers rather than interpret the stories for them. In the same spirit, because the pleasures of reading are inseparable from the surprises, secrets and revelations that all narratives contain, we strongly advise you to enjoy this book before turning to the Introduction.

General Adviser
KEITH CARABINE
Rutherford College
University of Kent at Canterbury

INTRODUCTION

I

For many readers *Ethan Frome* is the most intense and painful of all Edith Wharton's fictions, but for Wharton herself it was the tale which gave her 'the greatest joy and the fullest ease' in its writing.[1] Although she claimed to be 'bored and even exasperated' (*ABG*, p. 209) when told that it was her best book, she looked back on it as the work where she first 'suddenly felt the artisan's full control of his implements' (*ABG*, p. 209), and she defended it, lifelong, against

---

1 Wharton, *A Backward Glance* (p. 293) (hereafter *ABG*). Whenever possible, I use only the author's name to identify a title. For full details of this and other references, turn to 'A Selective Bibliography' at the end of this Introduction. I should like to thank Keith Carabine and Ben Knights for their helpful comments on this Introduction.

criticism. By 1911, when *Ethan Frome* appeared, Wharton could hardly have been called an apprentice. She had been publishing steadily since 1899 (*Ethan Frome* was her sixteenth book in thirteen years); she was well known for her writings on travel and archi-tecture, and famous for her short-story collections and her novels (*The House of Mirth* had been the runaway American bestseller of 1905). But for Wharton, as for many of her readers since, *Ethan Frome* plainly represented something different, particularly compel-ling for both its subject matter, and for its technical challenges. Following Lewis's lead, critics have often read the book as coded autobiography, seeing in the central relationships a dark reflection of Edith Wharton's own recently ended love affair with the journalist Morton Fullerton and her final troubled years with her husband, Teddy, a neurotic and demanding invalid. (The marriage was ended by divorce in 1913.) But Wharton had another, peculiarly intense, affair with the region where the tale was set. She had regarded Western Massachusetts as her real home since 1902, when she and Teddy had moved into the Mount, a magnificent country house in Lenox, designed to Wharton's exacting specifications. In her auto-biography, Wharton described life in the country as 'the only state which has always completely satisfied me' (*ABG*, p. 124); and for nearly a decade on acquiring the Mount, she had spent most summers in New England, writing, overseeing her wonderful gardens, enter-taining friends, and exploring the Berkshire mountains in her chauffeur-driven motor. By the time she wrote *Ethan Frome*, these years were nearly over. With her marriage deteriorating, Wharton made no visits during 1909 or 1910; reluctantly, she reached the decision to put the house on the market, and it was sold in September 1911, the month *Ethan Frome* was published.

Whenever Wharton discussed the book, as in *A Backward Glance* or in her Introduction to the 1922 edition (included here), she saw it as embodying the essence of New England as she felt she had come to understand it. By the 1890s, Lenox had become a favourite retreat for wealthy summer visitors, marked out by Baedeker for its air of luxury, but Wharton intended to counter the idealised tourist images, per-petuated, she felt, by 'Local Colour' fiction. For years, she claimed, she had wanted to reveal the truth about life in the derelict, half-deserted mountain villages she had glimpsed in her travels – remote even in her time, unthinkably isolated 'before the coming of motor and telephone' (*ABG*, p. 296). Here, 'insanity, incest and slow mental and moral starvation were hidden away behind the paintless wooden house-fronts'. While Emily Brontë would have found 'as savage tragedies [here] . . . as on her Yorkshire moors', American writers, Wharton thought, had done the reality of the area little justice (*ABG*, pp. 294, 294). Her predecessors, regional writers such as Mary Wilkins [Freeman] and Sarah Orne Jewett, had ignored the 'outcropping granite' (p. 29) for the superficial picturesque scene. Although modern readers now find in such writers a bleaker vision than the 'rose-and-lavender' (*ABG*, p. 294) sentimentality Wharton condemned, she clearly believed that they offered too cosy a view. For her, these were 'grim places' (*ABG*, p. 294) which demanded more stringent literary treatment; and in 1910, in an interval from her struggles with the ambitious canvas of *The Custom of the Country*, she turned to work on a restricted group of characters in a remote Western Massachusetts setting, worlds away from the crowded panoramas of her society fiction.

In choosing her subject, Wharton was revisiting a situation she had begun to develop in an unfinished piece some years before. Oddly, for what would become her 'most effectively American work' (Lewis, p. 309), this was a story written in French as a language exercise. Spending a winter in Paris (according to Lewis, probably in 1907), Wharton had arranged sessions with a young tutor to polish her conversational French. The lessons at an end, she forgot about the sketch, but 'a few years later Ethan's history stirred again in my memory' , and she began to write her tale in English.[2] The brief ' "Gallic Ethan" ' (which Wharton believed lost) sets up the central triangle of relationships between Hart (Ethan), Anna (Zeena) and Mattie, her cousin, and treats the episode of Anna's trip to consult a new doctor, and the banishing of Mattie on her return. The sketch ends at the station, as Hart sees Mattie on to the train. He vows to go with her; she insists that he must stay in his unhappy marriage: Anna had given her a home after her father's death, and Mattie refuses to shame her or to disgrace herself. In reviving the story, Wharton retained some details, but expanded and complicated it. On the one hand, she heightened the action, by taking it onwards to the dramatic sledding ride at its climax. (It is generally assumed that she based this incident on a coasting catastrophe still recent in Lenox memory. The local press had given full coverage to the horrific crash on Courthouse Hill, where a 'double-ripper' sled

2 Wharton, 'The Writing of *Ethan Frome*'. The manuscript survives among Wharton's papers, held in the Beinecke Library, Yale University; it was published, with a commentary, by MacCallan.

ran into a lamp-post, killing an eighteen-year-old high-school girl and leaving her four companions badly injured. Although Wharton was in Europe at the time, she is now known to have befriended one of the survivors, who worked in the local library.)[3] On the other hand, however, she distanced her story, adding the frame narrative, the twenty-four-year gap in time and the unnamed first-person narrator, so crucial to the tale's effects.

Wharton later remembered the exercise-book beginnings of *Ethan Frome* as a 'singular accident' (*ABG*, p. 295) which fixed its conception uniquely in her mind; working on the tale again, as her writing progressed, she exclaimed over her project as an awkward child, referring to it typically in a tone of defensive affection. Too long for a short story, but too short for a novel, it had become 'that ridiculous nouvelle, which has grown into a large long-legged hobbledoy of a young novel. 20,000 long it is already, and growing. I have to let its frocks down every day, and soon it will be in trousers!'[4] Anticipating his disappointment, she apologised for the book to Bernard Berenson: it was 'only an anecdote in 45,000 words', destined for publication in 'a volumelet'.[5] She was right to predict disapproval: when *Ethan Frome* appeared, as a *Scribner's Magazine* serial in August to October 1911, and as a book in September, the praise it received seemed offset by its comparatively slow sales at the start – just over four thousand by the end of November, seven thousand by February 1912 (Lewis, p. 311). When Wharton complained about what seemed unsatisfactory figures, her publisher, Charles Scribner, pointed out that fiction of a non-standard length was always unpopular and unprofitable. (Years afterwards in her epic *Hudson River Bracketed* [1929], Wharton satirised him as the publisher Mr Dreck, an insensitive philistine, who 'didn't know a meaner length' for a book than forty-five thousand words.)

Reviewers, too, seemed uncertain how to define the work (a novel, a short story, a 'short long story',[6] or even a drama); but most found its narrative extraordinarily compelling. Even those who felt its situation sordid or its ending too cruel admired its subtlety and its concentration. Like a short story, it could be read at a sitting,

3 For details, see Marshall.
4 Wharton, January 4 (1911), *Letters*, ed. Lewis (p. 232)
5 May 16 (1911), *Letters* (p. 240)
6 *Outlook* 99 (21 October 1911): 4. For a range of reviews, see Tuttleton, Lauer and Murray; samples may also be found on-line, through the Edith Wharton Society website.

building its effects detail by detail; like Greek tragedy, it sustained
an uninterrupted, inevitable movement to its stunning climax and
revelation. These qualities clearly survived being encountered in
the serial form: to Wharton's pleasure, Henry James praised its
'beautiful artful *kept-downness*, & yet effective cumulation' (Powers,
p. 195) although she regretted that he had not read the story first in
the single volume. *Ethan Frome* has lost none of its force for readers
since. Today it is one of the best known of all Wharton's writings, a
favourite with teachers and anthologists as well as the object of
intense critical debate, and it has been widely translated and
variously adapted for new audiences. In 1936, Wharton, though
too frail to travel to the United States to see the play itself, wrote an
enthusiastic preface to the script of a successful theatrical version
and more recently the story has been reworked again for opera,
television and film.[7]

How to classify the book remains a problem. Wharton herself
referred to *Ethan Frome* as a 'tale', a 'story', a 'novel', a 'short-novel'
and, in Henry James's expression, a 'nouvelle'; and the book is listed
in indexes today under similarly diverse categories. For many critics
now, however, 'nouvelle' (or 'novella') seems a belittling term; and
when applied to fiction by a woman writer, it might seem to suggest
a product less robust and significant than the work of her fellow
male artists. Katherine Anne Porter forcefully dismissed the word,
enjoining her own readers in 1965:

> [P]lease do not call my short novels *Novelettes*, or even worse,
> *Novellas*. Novelette is classical usage for a trivial, dime-novel sort
> of thing; Novella is a slack, boneless, affected word that we do not
> need to describe anything. Please call my works by their right
> names: we have four that cover every division: short stories, long
> stories, short novels, novels.   [p. xvi]

Nevertheless, especially when used in its period context, 'novella'
describes a literary form with a rich history. Many of the most
commanding works of Wharton's contemporaries (among them,
Conrad, James, Lawrence, Harding Davis, Chopin, Gilman) are

---

7 *Ethan Frome* (American Playhouse Theatrical Films and Miramax Films,
   1993), directed by John Madden, screenplay by Richard Nelson. The cast
   included Liam Neeson as Ethan, Patricia Arquette as Mattie, Joan Allen as
   Zenobia, and Tate Donovan as 'Reverend Smith' (a new minister to the
   district, substituted by Richard Nelson for the unnamed engineer narrator).

novellas, and Wharton herself had already successfully attempted
the form in some of her most powerful early fictions: 'Bunner
Sisters' (written in 1892), *The Touchstone* (1900), *Sanctuary* (1903)
and *Madame de Treymes* (1907). Intensity and concentration, so
central to the effects of *Ethan Frome*, seem particularly characteristic
of the type, as also are the elliptical devices of the frame narrative,
the unnamed narrator, the delayed disclosure, hinted at in an array of
details, and the sharpened sense of an ending as time materially runs
out. With all this in mind, then, the reader may well feel that
'novella' (or even 'nouvelle') may, after all, be the most fitting term.

II

Ethan Frome is an outsider's story: a reconstruction of an episode in
the past, guessed at by a stranger, and of a life in a small, shuttered
community glimpsed from a distance. Sensing difficulties with
perspective, Wharton adopted what for her were unusual narrative
strategies. As her 1922 Introduction tells us, she defined her
problems as a set of technical challenges, to do with the bridging of
gaps. She had to find an approach to handling the lapse in time
between her tragedy's 'first acts' and its 'dramatic . . . anti-climax' a
generation later; and she needed to negotiate the space between the
way her rural characters experienced life ('starkly and summarily')
and the depiction of these feelings in art ('any attempt to elaborate
and complicate their sentiments would necessarily have falsified the
whole', p. 29). Wharton's solution was to pursue her subject much
along the lines described by Henry James in one of his recently
published Prefaces: 'to follow it as much from its outer edge in,
rather than from its centre outward'.[8] Using the device of the
narrative frame and the voice of the first-person narrator (a tactic
she reserved otherwise for short stories), she divided the viewpoint,
between Ethan in the main chapters and the narrator in the frame.
In this way, she could present both the immediate intensity of
experience and the reflective speculation she had thought mutually
exclusive. Splitting the action, she plunged her readers back into
the tense drama of Ethan's story a quarter of a century before; and,
at the same time, played her trick of half-revelation, producing her
most shocking exposure almost as a casual afterword as she returns
us to the present. (Wharton often keeps secrets, but this is one for
which many readers have hardly been able to forgive her.)

8   Preface to 'The Author of Beltraffio', 'The Middle Years', etc. (1909), p. 1238

Wharton's worries about structure hint at the deeper ones of her own relation to her material. In her society fiction, she was thoroughly at home with the manners and register of her fashionable cosmopolitans. Although she had experimented with a New England location (an industrial town) in *The Fruit of the Tree* (1907), there she had given all her main characters genteel connections. In *Ethan Frome*, however, writing of New England country people, she was attempting a language in some ways more alien to her than the idiomatic French in which she had started. Here, she was trying to enter the inner life of a landscape through which she had passed only as a privileged observer. Wharton vigorously denied any difficulty. As we have seen, she took pains to emphasise her credentials – her ten-year residence in the hills and her familiarity with the locals' dialect and outlook – and she expressed only pleasure in the enterprise. Working on her novella in Paris, she clearly enjoyed recreating a landscape a world away: 'The scene is laid at Starkfield, Mass, and the nearest cosmopolis is called Shadd's Falls. It amuses me to do that décor in the rue de Varenne.'[9] To some, the 'décor' might suggest caricature, the creation of a piece of rural grotesque, closer to theatrical melodrama (or, later, to Stella Gibbons's parodic Starkadder Farm), than a revelation of country life 'as it really was' (*ABG*, p. 293). Much to Wharton's vexation, some reviewers, finding similar notes in the text, raised problems of authenticity or, worse, suggested that she wrote in the 'unconsciously contemptuous key of the person who has a box at the opera' (Sergeant) and who could never hope to understand the realities of these lives. In trying to avoid a sentimental picture, had Wharton fallen instead into the opposite extreme? Were her descriptions of the monochrome interiors of the Frome household and the Frome marriage too unrelentingly bleak? her picture of the miseries and the meagre pleasures of country people merely the view of an onlooker repelled by the lives of those in a narrower world than her own? Or, conversely, did the more lyrical, passionate beauty of her novella idealise aspects of Starkfield in ways not so far from the tradition she sought to criticise?

We can never entirely dispel such queries about the ambiguities of *Ethan Frome*'s stance. To a degree, Wharton's devices do, indeed, seem to perpetuate 'Local Colour' versions of country life as either idyllic or brutal. In such narratives, popular in the late nineteenth-

9 January 4 (1911), *Letters* (p. 232)

century United States, a sophisticated urban observer typically frames for his similarly educated readers a picture of backward rural exotics living in cultural isolation. Even where the scene is romanticised, it is always tinged with condescension. The articulate visitor remains superior to the silent figures in the landscape whose stories he tells; their dignity emerges only as he interprets them for us; he exists in time, they remain in the realm of the picturesque. *Ethan Frome* contains many of these features. Wharton's metropolitan and enquiring narrator recounts his experience of a remote and reticent community. He details for his (implicitly more stylish) audience these people's ceremonies, social shadings and markers of status ('the "best parlour", with its black horsehair and mahogany', p. 36) and carefully transcribes their dialect. The district's past interests him still more than its present. An engineer, up-to-date with developments in science and technology, he is clearly intrigued, all the same, by the idea of a world untouched by modernity (before 'the degenerate days of trolley, bicycle and rural delivery'). Looking back, he is openly appalled by the sense of life's 'negation' a generation earlier (p. 35), but seems, at the same time, fascinated by a vision of an elemental kind of nobility (Wharton's *'granite outcroppings'*, p. 29) unknown in these more decadent times.

Most readers, however, find Wharton's approach far more complex. Her narrative-frame offers no secure overview or easy judgements, from opera-box or anywhere else. The experience of reading *Ethan Frome* undermines any schematic contrasts between past and present, country and city, nature and culture, or between frame and inset story, or the narrator and those whose lives he interprets. The novella's close leaves us with little sense that we now know the definitive story, 'the clue to Ethan Frome' (p. 42), or are even certain whose story we have been reading, or what kind of tale it is. Should it be read within or as a critique of the regional tradition (see Campbell); as a piece of social realism with Darwinian underpinning; or in other ways altogether? perhaps as a myth, a devastating vision of 'unrelenting infertility' (Waid)? or as a fairy-tale, a feminist *Snow-White*, a warning against a culture that turns its women into witches (Ammons)? Few critics, these included, would propose consigning *Ethan Frome* to any rigid category; indeed, much of the most interesting debate about the text has centred on its intricacy, the coexistence of different and contradictory elements. Rather than attempting to settle interpretation, then, it seems more productive to examine some of the cross-lights and uncertainties which draw us back to rereading.

III

Many of the complications emanate from Wharton's narrator. In choosing to introduce the region through a first-person voice, Wharton risked, as we have seen, all the problems associated with making a cultivated man who can express himself tell the story of a social inferior who cannot. But she also took care not to make that voice seem authoritative. Aware, perhaps, in spite of her denials, that she could never hope to represent the Starkfield community from within as she had her New Yorkers, she created an intermediary who brings issues of interpretation into the foreground. Her narrator has no claims to special insights. From first to last, he (like the reader) remains an onlooker who strains to hear and to understand ('his words never reached me', p. 34; 'I put the case anew to my village oracle . . . but got for my pains only a uncomprehending grunt', p. 36). In her twin New England short novel *Summer* (1917), my 'Hot Ethan' as she called it (Lewis, p. 396), Wharton dispensed with the device, but there too she refused the reader access at some of the most significant points of the narrative: *Summer* ends with a closed door which shuts us out of any certain knowledge about the characters' motivation and gives no assurances about their future.

From the very first sentence of *Ethan Frome*, Wharton never allows us to forget that we are reading a partial version, a reconstruction of a buried story. (She credited Balzac and Browning for her fragmented method [p. 31], but readers will also be reminded of *Wuthering Heights* and critics have made comparisons with Hawthorne, James and Conrad.) Her narrator pieces his information together 'bit by bit, from various people' (p. 33), eager to get a complete account, tracking 'missing facts' (p. 36), but sensing, all the same, that the 'deeper meaning of the story was in the gaps' (p. 34). The text, as Blackall points out, make these gaps visible. Wharton wanted to highlight the main divisions of the narrative (on pages 42, 110 and 112) with a definite typographical sign, even more marked than the lines of dots the editor eventually chose. It is in these breaks, and in the shorter ellipses elsewhere, Blackall argues, that Wharton gives readers room for their own initiatives. As Fryer suggests, a female reader might imagine a version very different from the narrator's – Zeena's tragedy, perhaps: 'What must it be like to be Zenobia, a woman imprisoned on an isolated farm with only the taciturn and inarticulate Ethan for company?' (p. 182).[10] In turn, perhaps, Wharton's spaces tactfully leave the characters some independence. They are not to be contained within a single account, an outsider's viewpoint. The narrator puts together one 'vision' (p. 42) of Ethan's story, but the closing frame undercuts any sense of completeness, or even that he has found the 'key' (p. 36) he sought. Mrs Hale's revelations are only partial; she cuts off Mattie's crucial secret in another tantalising blank ('she [. . .] looked straight at me out of her big eyes, and said . . . ', p. 113) and she resists pretending she can read Zeena ('I never knew myself what Zeena thought – I don't to this day', p. 113).

If the text always allows for alternative versions, it also invites us, similarly, to reread seemingly mundane surfaces, to think about the 'huge cloudy meanings behind the daily face of things' (p. 43). As always in Wharton's fiction, objects speak volumes. Some, like the much discussed red glass pickle-dish, carry an obvious symbolic and emotional freight: Mattie's ruin of Zeena's unused 'treasure' (p. 89) focuses all the waste, frustration and sexual tension of the novel, and devastatingly prefigures the further breakages to come. (See Waid, Bernard, Beer Goodwyn and Singley for examples of especially sensitive readings.) The fragile dish is a gift (a wedding present to Zeena, a delicate tribute from Mattie to Ethan), one of several in this short text. Gifts, as Wharton knew from her readings in anthropology, transmit promises, imply possibilities or assert power-relations and alliances, and they are always significant in her fiction. In *Ethan Frome*, references to pots of geraniums guarded against the winter, a 'box covered with fancy paper' (p. 75), or a hard cushion 'with strange protuberances' (p. 92), express more about the characters' emotional histories (and their possible futures) than would any overt narratorial commentary. But even passing references to other items ('a streak of crimson ribbon', p. 68, a 'broken-nosed milk-jug', p. 111, 'a calendar with "Thoughts from the Poets" ', p. 91) ask us to reconstruct the stories behind them. In *The Age of Innocence* (1920), Wharton's main characters contemplate a museum case, filled with the 'recovered fragments of Ilium', 'small broken objects – hardly recognisable domestic utensils, ornaments and personal trifles'.[11] Whatever we read in the trifles of *Ethan Frome* – hopes, lost chances, disappointed ambition, 'the hard compulsions of the poor' (p. 113) – like the narrator, we always

10 For Fryer and others, a fate with echoes of Nathaniel Hawthorne's tragic heroine of *The Blithedale Romance* (1852)

suspect that what we imagine conceals further stories beyond; that there is always space for other readings.

One of the tale's most teasing 'gaps' is the narrator himself. Wharton makes it hard, even impossible, to decide on his exact status in the text. We are not told his name, his family history, or even gender (though it would be a surprise to find a woman engineer in an early 1900s' novel; and most of Wharton's narrators, as Nettels reminds us, are professional men). This vagueness allows us to regard him as a mere mechanism, if we wish, even to forget him entirely for most of the narrative and to concentrate on the passions of Ethan, Zeena and Mattie. After the preliminary pages, the central nine chapters are related in the third-person, with no intrusive reminders of his presence. However, it is equally possible to feel that his voice and vision command the story, colouring everything we read. His laconic, direct, oral address in the opening ('If you know Starkfield, Massachusetts, you know the post-office', p. 34) seems to promise a plain tale of events and consequences, the story of the 'smash-up', not the intensely wrought inner drama that follows; but both are equally memorable, and more so, when read in conjunction. Many critics have been interested in his perceptions, in how the two parts of his narrative fit together, and particularly in what happens as he crosses the threshold into the Frome family story. Wharton always sensed the threshold as a place of threat or transformation, for, as Banta reminds us, 'we do not know we have crossed [it] until after the crucial moment recedes into the past' (p. 6). Wolff, most notably, makes out a forceful argument for regarding its significance here as confirming the narrator as the book's actual subject, and Ethan Frome (as he appears in the inner story) as *'no more than a figment of the narrator's imagination'* (Wolff, p. 164). For her, the novella is a psychological study. We cross the 'line of light' (p. 42) into an extended 'dream vision' (Wolff, p. 165) where the narrator projects his darkest fears on to the blank figure of Ethan. As we read the central chapters back into the frame, gaining 'a glimpse into the most appalling recesses of the narrator's mind', we encounter a 'shadow self' (Wolff, pp. 165, 184) in flight from adult realities, sexual commitment, self-assertion.

11 Wharton, *Novels*, ed. Lewis, pp. 1261, 1262

IV

Few readers, perhaps, would want to give the narrator so much priority, or collapse the entire text into the abyss of a single mind; and Wharton's own commentary assumes the objective 'truth' (p. 30) of her tragedy, suggesting that her main difficulty was only how he could, convincingly, get hold of the actual story. Nevertheless, Wolff's account is stimulating, not least in emphasising how Wharton unsettles easy assumptions about which, if any, narrative is dominant, and in calling attention to the sense of compulsive absorption with which the narrator is drawn to his subject. For the incomer, Ethan Frome is the most 'striking' and most taciturn of the ' "natives" ' (p. 33). The engineer plays the hunter, setting snares for Ethan's story. Failing to lure him to speech with questions, 'slight pleasantries', or even the gift of a volume of popular science, he can only resort to guesses based on his 'inflection . . . and his . . . silence' (p. 38). At the same time, trying to piece the truth together, he acts as an archaeologist, an antiquarian, intent on reconstructing a broken monument from a vanished past. (Wharton's own writing can often be seen as a similar enterprise.) Fascinated, he reads Ethan as a 'ruin of a man', cast in metal rather than flesh, glimpsing in him the traces of something uniquely powerful, archaic and elemental. Even Ethan's cap is 'helmet-like' (p. 37), his profile 'the bronze image of a hero' seen in relief against the snow; set apart from the community, he seems beyond the human, identical with the spirit of place, 'a part of the mute melancholy landscape, an incarnation of its frozen woe' (p. 38). In the banal present, the narrator introduces him at the post-office, with its neat brick pavement and white colonnade, but elsewhere, in the depths of his 'vision' (p. 42), he suggests his true element, placing him against grander backgrounds, the 'sky of iron' where 'Orion flashed his cold fires' (p. 43), or the snow where 'the bluish cones caught in its surface stood out like ornaments of bronze' (p. 102).

Such moments are part of a larger pattern in the narrator's text, his constant interest in rendering a visual scene. Wharton gives him the eye of a painter. Many of *Ethan Frome*'s most memorable moments are pictures, framed within a frame: Ethan's glimpse through the window of Mattie in the dance; the repeated scenes, of Zeena, then Mattie, in the doorway, divided into almost cubist planes by the upward beam of the lantern (these passages were present even in the early French draft). Elsewhere, the narrator fills his canvas with impressionist records of colour and light, the subtle effects of clouds and winds. He records the minutiae (the 'intricate lace-like patterns' [p. 102] of wood-animals' tracks) and the magnificent changes of the sky and sun, the 'deep well of blue' behind the stars, the moon burning 'a gold-edged rent in the clouds' (p. 67). These are winter landscapes, sensitively registering every nuance of the snow, recreating for us, as in a third dimension, the absolute density of the cold in all its manifestations.[12] In the present, the narrator gives most attention to the deadening expanses of late winter. His characteristic images are of diffusion, greyness, wateriness and a pervading lack of definition; even the climactic blizzard that leads him to Ethan's secret 'seemed to be a part of the thickening darkness, to be the winter night itself descending on us layer by layer' (p. 41), obscuring not revealing. After the drabness of the frame, the first chapters of Ethan's drama emerge in sharp relief. The narrator heightens the country of the past, unfolding Ethan's flaring passions in a world of extremes, vibrant with colour and contrasts: 'darkly blue' shadows, 'white and scintillating fields', the winter morning 'clear as crystal' (p. 57). This is a radiant land of pure, glowing cold, burning skies, spangled light.

In Mattie's sphere, colours intensify. Her presence is typically marked by vivid touches of brilliance – the cherry-coloured 'fascinator', the 'streak of crimson ribbon', the blueberries and the dish 'of gay red glass' (p. 68); Ethan sees her face as 'part of the sun's red and of the pure glitter on the snow' (p. 57); and senses her in images of summer (a stream, a breeze), birds in flight, happiness felt in 'flashes . . . as if they had surprised a butterfly in the winter woods' (p. 102). With Zeena, all colour drains down. She emerges through a muted palette of greys, blacks and browns, within dull interiors or as a presence behind closed doors, a darkly brooding air of 'hints and menaces' (p. 49). Even absent, she exerts a chilling blight; and her final appearance in the inner story is a hideous vision, a face 'with twisted monstrous lineaments' which 'thrust itself' (p. 109) between Ethan and his goal. Her miasma infects the present. The horror of the final section is, in part, heightened by the nightmarish sense of sound. With the small, frightened 'twittering' (p. 109) still echoing, we enter the nightmare of 'knowing that the querulous droning voice we hear at the end of the narrator's introduction is that of the bright and vivacious Mattie Silver at the beginning of the story'

---

12 Similar winter effects on canvas were a speciality of some turn-of-the-century American Impressionists, most notably, the painter John Henry Twatchman (1853–1902), and his pupil Ernest Lawson (1873–1939). Nat Fulmer in Wharton's *The Glimpses of the Moon* (1922) is a painter of this school.

(Fryer, p. 192). But the shock is also of stasis, rendered through the sudden reduction of colour. Zeena is recognisably herself, pale, opaque and sallow; but Mattie now mirrors her, her hair 'as grey as her companion's, her face as bloodless and shrivelled' (p. 110). Worse, her glow lingers, grotesquely transformed, in her 'amber-tinted' skin, her dark, 'bright witch-like stare' (p. 110).

In the narrator's terrible vision, Zeena exerts a strange dark energy. Her sour resentment grows into an active malignity, that seems beyond the human. She is a witch, complete with lurking cat as her familiar (Ammons); a 'living ghost' (Fedorko, p. 65) out of a Gothic 'vault' (p. 55); or, even more powerfully, an 'exacting Calvinist God bent on condemnation and retribution' (Singley, p. 121). The narrator loads the story against her, typing the two women, as do so many of Wharton's male characters, in terms of opposites. Mattie seems composed of a charming whirl of feminine contra-dictions, seen in adjacent paragraphs, with a wrist 'no bigger than a child's' but as 'womanly in shape and motion' (p. 68). Zeena, in the parallel scene, is 'angular', a creature from 'the last dream before waking' (p. 55), rendered in a disconnected sequence of ugly parts: a flat breast, a puckered throat, fantastical hollows and prominences and a ring of crimping pins. The one is a 'fascinator', all warmth, quicksilver, blushes, laughter and animation, the other a serpent 'shooting venom' (p. 83), a Gorgon who paralyses and freezes. Mattie inspires Ethan to speech; Zeena silences him. Mattie restores the 'springs' of his masculinity (Bernard, p. 69): 'Except when he was steering a big log down the mountain to his mill he had never known such a thrilling sense of mastery' (p. 71). Zeena emasculates him.[13]

In this set of contrasts, Mattie represents romantic escape, Zeena imprisonment; but, again, Wharton complicates matters. The two women begin to blur in Ethan's, and the narrator's, imaginations long before the dreadful revelation of the ending:

> As her young brown head detached itself against the patchwork cushion that habitually framed his wife's gaunt countenance, Ethan had a momentary shock. It was almost as if the other face, the face of the superseded woman, had obliterated that of the intruder.   [p. 71]

13 The images of bitter pickles and the dead cucumber vine have given critics much to ponder: for Waid, these are 'emblems of a lost or past fertility' (p. 75), for Bernard (pp. 66–8), and for Singley (p. 120), a withering association of masculinity with sterility and disease.

This picture of Mattie framed in Zeena's rocking-chair is one of the most disquieting in the text. It occurs at a point of deepest intimacy, just when Ethan's 'dream' seems to be coming true. He has the sense of 'being in another world, where all was warmth and harmony and time could bring no change' (p. 72). In Wharton, this state is always a fantasy. Here, no woman means freedom. As Ethan glimpses, all merge into one, locking men into reality: first Ethan's mother, then Zeena (Ethan 'wondered if Zeena were also turning "queer". Women did, he knew' [p. 64]), then Mattie. Even she would have been followed, as she senses, by the new hired girl who would 'sleep in my bed, where I used to lay nights' (p. 107). There are also more spectral beings: Endurance Frome and the other women 'down in the graveyard' (p. 114), and the 'stricken creatures' of the neigh-bourhood in the lonely farmhouses 'where sudden tragedy had come of their presence' (p. 64). As Mrs Hale suggests, Ethan's women kill him, even Mattie: 'if she'd ha' died, Ethan might ha' lived' (p. 114).

The most positive models of fulfilment in the text are in male worlds: in science, technology and books, the study which is Ethan's 'refuge' (p. 91), set out as a shrine to the life of the mind and spirit. Ethan's aspirations, achieved by the narrator, were 'to live in towns, where there were lectures and big libraries and "fellows doing things" ' (p. 63). Women bring him back to the country, the land, the home and the body. A number of critics (Ammons, Fedorko, Fryer, Waid and Wolff, for example) have traced such repetitions in detail. These patterns point, they suggest, to the narrator's, and possibly Ethan's, fears about, variously, mothers, wives, sexuality, 'woman', or 'femininity and masculinity' in general (Farland and Fedorko). Most of these critics, however, question how far such misogyny extends to Wharton's text as a whole. Many readers have made out (as we saw Fryer doing above) a sympathetic case for all these women, prisoners themselves of loneliness, lack of opportu-nity, physical hardship, minimal education, poverty, destructive dependency. ' "Ethan, where'll I go if I leave you? I don't know how to get along alone" ' (p. 107), Mattie asks; Zeena rallies, not because she has won some dark victory, but because she responds to a crisis, and has important work to do.

V

Looking at such aspects of the text takes us out of broadly psycho-analytical readings into *Ethan Frome*'s evocation of a specific culture. Wharton does not date any of the events precisely, and leaves it unclear just how long her narrator has waited to tell his story. Writing about 'the outcropping granite' (p. 29), she draws our inward eye, with Mattie's, to the movements of the stars or 'the huge panorama of the ice age, and the long dim stretches of succeeding time' (p. 46). All this might suggest her lack of interest in locating the tale in history, conjuring up, instead, the air of a timeless pastoral, or a sense of scale so vast as to make the present insignificant. But looking back to the 1880s from the early 1900s, the text is attuned to details of a particular region on the cusp of change. The narrator's plunge out of time and progress is caused by a thoroughly contemporary phenomenon, a strike at the power-house by the carpenters, then one of the most powerful labour groups. The narrative, as a whole, is concerned with conflicts of interest, shifts in power-relations, and in immediate and rapid historical transitions, underlined in its numerous allusions to evolving technologies and economies. Although Starkfield is isolated, it is connected to larger histories and geographies. The references to real places, farther and farther distant (Springfield, Worcester, Florida or even 'the West', p. 92), and to the complicated arrangements for journeys on which much of the action hinges, remind us of social worlds elsewhere.

In working on *The Custom of the Country* (temporarily laid aside), Wharton was exploring the impact of rising 'new money' on older leisure-class social strata. In *Ethan Frome*, too, she is fascinated by the effects of energies from outside on a formerly self-sufficient culture. Here, the centres of influence are the growing towns, places of capital and enterprise, whether expressed in the references to department stores or to modish doctors. Opening the novella at the post-office, where Ethan collects Zeena's envelopes, Wharton takes us directly into a significant contact point where city retail penetrated new rural markets, part of the dramatic 'modernisation' of the country from the 1870s onwards (Schlereth, p. 339). The text alludes to a spectrum of invaders, from rural electrification to consumer goods and novel forms of leisure (by the 1900s, the theatre and the YMCA rather than the local dance and the church picnic). Even in Ethan's youth, the signs of Gilded Age aspiration are everywhere: in the Eady's new brick grocery built on '"smart" business methods' (p. 45); the snatches of slang or fashion (in terms often set apart in quotation marks); the jokes about the grand piano and the 'cupolo' (p. 65) for the farmhouse; the newspapers with their 'seductive' (p. 93) advertising sheets; the mail-order goods; the expensive patent medicines which drain the Frome economies. Zeena's useless 'electric battery' (p. 59), which costs an astonishing twenty dollars, combines nearly all of these. From the late 1870s, marketing the mysteries of 'electrical medicine' became a hugely attractive commercial prospect. When even US congressmen recharged their exhausted brainpower with electrical apparatus in the cellar of the Capitol building (Nye, p. 153), it was easy to promise miracles to hopeful new customers in the provinces.

The extraordinarily varied modes of transport mentioned in the text (from horse-drawn sleigh to stage-coach to trolley-car) register another of the most important forces. The coming of the railroad, which is such a significant feature in the story, reshaped the landscape of Massachusetts from the 1840s. It opened up and transformed the larger towns mentioned in the text, drawing 'the smart ones' (p. 35) to the new business and industrial centres (see Brooke, pp. 307, 390), but leaving other areas, as Ethan expresses it, 'kinder side-tracked here now' (p. 41). By the late nineteenth-century, suburban town-dwellers were viewing this 'rusticated rural New England' (Clark, p. 329) in the idealised images which would turn regions such as the Berkshires into a perfect Baedeker tourist landscape. Acquiring the Mount, Wharton herself was a beneficiary, travelling in her own private motor, a privileged form of transport, too advanced even for a reference in the text. Yet, though she celebrated 'the deep joy of communion with the earth', and the happy drives through 'that loveliest region' (*AGB*, pp. 124, 125), it was these images she set out to dispel. Her text makes us aware of the moment, and of its ambiguities. For all the beauty of the hills, they are never simply scenery. The region is gripped in a cycle of economic decline. Though increasingly dependent on the money economy of the cities, this is a place where actual cash is scarce. In his twenties, Ethan cannot muster a fare to the West; in his fifties, 'he wouldn't be sorry to earn a dollar' (p. 37). The land is starved and unproductive, the farm unsellable, Ethan's sawmill redundant with the arrival of new technologies (Gschwend). Even the picturesque New England farmhouse is unaffordable. As the narrator muses, Ethan has been forced to remove the indigenous 'L', the 'actual hearthstone' of the home, with all its 'symbolic' resonance – not least for the town visitor 'the image it presents of a life linked with the soil' (p. 40).

Although the cities hold out alternative possibilities, in this narrative these are seldom realised. All three members of the Frome household are victims. Mattie's father had succeeded in 'descending from the hills to Connecticut', marrying into a 'thriving drug business' (p. 58); but his failure (mismanaged 'smart' methods) leaves

Mattie useless after a fashionably genteel education. She is neither a modern city girl (she fails at stenography and work in a department store), nor a competent old-fashioned hand around the farmhouse. Zeena, too, is caught between worlds; she clings to a residual sense of community, afraid to lose her status in a larger town, but has no sphere for action on an isolated farm, farther from the railway than her larger 'native village' (p. 63).

VI

If the text gives most space to Ethan, it is because for the narrator his tragedy comes closest. As we have seen, their affinities strike most critics, from a common interest in scientific progress to memories of visiting Florida; and it is in Ethan's former study that the narrator sleeps on the night of his vision. As in Lockwood's haunted night in the oak closet at Wuthering Heights, he is in a spot charged for his host with a peculiarly intense and intimate history, a place where minds and souls might meet. [14] The narrator shares, too, some of Wharton's own ambiguities in relation to the region, which link him more uneasily with Ethan's failure. With 'a job connected with the big power-house' (p. 35), like his author, though in a different manner, he represents some of the outside currents which are changing the countryside. He is a favourite early twentieth-century literary type: associated with engineering and electricity, a version of the Thomas Edison figure, like the hero of Willa Cather's *Alexander's Bridge* published in 1912, the following year. Forced to inertia, he is stimulated to 'creative zeal', like Wharton herself, by the 'country quiet' (*ABG*, p. 125), horrified and fascinated by the depths of silence he explores. One impulse of his story, as we have seen, is to place Ethan safely outside history and progress, as a hero made out of grander substance; but another is to acknowledge the appalling nullity of his life in this specific time, place and circumstance.

Ethan's story grows out of the silence. Both Wharton and her narrator contemplate the riddle of one whose 'flight' (p. 35) has been permanently hindered. Ethan's is the opposite of a life conducted through the power of the imagination to make things happen. For Edith Wharton, the Berkshires meant personal fulfilment, found

---

14 Emily Brontë, *Wuthering Heights* (1847), Chapter 3. In *The Fruit of the Tree*, too, Wharton used a small back room, with its books and pictures, as the place where Justine, her heroine, experiences a sense of direct contact with the thoughts and spirit of its owner.

through work: they gave her 'a new harvest of beauty', 'fields and woods of my own' (*ABG*, pp. 153, 124) that she could transform to her own designs. She modelled her house after an English stately home, Belton House in Lincolnshire (built in 1642),[15] and she styled her gardens along the lines she had described in her architectural guide, *Italian Villas and Their Gardens* (1904). In her views on landscape and interior design, Wharton always emphasised the necessity of private spaces; and she turned The Mount into a place where she could write. Much of the horror of *Ethan Frome* arises from the vision of lives spent 'all shut up there 'n that one kitchen' (p. 113); of the intimate marital bedroom Ethan is ashamed to enter in front of Mattie; of his attempts to keep his study separate, or to speak a private word. Worse still, is the vision that nobody can leave. Unlike those who tell his story, Ethan has no control over space and time, no money, no chance to work elsewhere. Wharton herself had the freedom to write her novella in France, to return to The Mount before its publication, and, no matter how reluctantly she made the decision, she could choose to move away, from the region and from her marriage. Her engineer aside, her characters have no such resources. Ethan's speech cannot reach the surface. In the narrator's reconstruction, Mattie allows Ethan to glimpse the wonders of simile ('It looks just as if it was painted!' p. 46), but he does not break through to eloquence: 'he groped for a dazzling phrase, and brought out, in a growl of rapture: "Come along"' (p. 52). Writing the letter that might transform his life, his pen halts; knowing that he has communicated his dream to Mattie gives him a 'thrill of joy' (p. 104), but the letter ends in shreds and he has no real faith in the power of writing: 'Oh, what good'll writing do?' (p. 104).

If the novella is a kind of ghost story, as various critics have viewed it, among its most haunting effects are the stories that do not happen. One of the most astonishing after-images of *Ethan Frome* is the sense of the alternative futures sketched in potential points of exit throughout the narrative. Although the suggestion of roads not taken is a property of many narratives, Wharton increases their effect here by making them part of the constant tension between visions of escape and certainty of imprisonment. In Wolff's reading, Ethan's history is the narrator's shadow-story, but there are many more, most of them arising out of Ethan's own dreads and desires:

15 For details, plans and photographs, see Dwight, Craig and, on-line, at The Mount website.

Mattie's marriage to Dennis Eady, Zeena's murder by tramps. Some suggest happy endings. If Ethan's fantasy of the fair child dressed like a princess comes close to sentimental cliché, the fate of the deserted wife seems closer to the kind of up-beat transformation found in Charlotte Perkins Gilman's stories for the feminist *Forerunner* (1909–16): she successfully sells the farm and blossoms running a lunch-room. In a later New England fiction, Robert Frost's poem 'The Star-Splitter', the failed hill-man himself breaks out of the cycle of 'hugger-mugger farming' to a kind of comic triumph. Entranced, like Ethan with Orion and the 'heavenly stars', 'He burned his house down for the fire insurance/ And spent the proceeds on a telescope/ To satisfy a life-long curiosity/ About our place in the infinities' (Frost, p. 202). In *Ethan Frome*, the repeated motifs of wonder, vision, of growth sustained through winter, of seeds (and even seed-catalogues) perhaps subtly encourage us to hope for a similar affirmative gesture. But Wharton always interrupts and frustrates the moment: 'The inexorable facts closed in on him like prison-warders handcuffing a convict' (p. 93), leaving us only with images of lives frozen, blasted and wasted.

Wharton saves her most powerful story until last, the dream of love-in-death in the climactic and long-deferred coasting ride. But *Ethan Frome* refuses narrator and reader even the consolations of a romantic tragedy. For all the emotional and erotic power of the final sledding-run, we know in advance that Ethan and Mattie will not die together in a 'long delirious descent' (p. 109). But the tale also resists the temptation to preserve the moment as a memory; the engineer and Ethan, contrary to one traditional narrative pattern, do not unite, mourning the death of a young and beautiful girl. Sleeping in Ethan's defunct study, perhaps even sharing his dreams, the narrator's vision leads us to the novel's most terrible ghosts. Even *Wuthering Heights*, in its closing words, allows Lockwood, its main narrator, to lay to rest the spirits he has seen, to wonder 'how anyone could ever imagine unquiet slumbers for the sleepers in that quiet earth'. Wharton, too, leaves us with a vision of the Fromes 'up at the farm' and 'the Fromes down in the graveyard', but locked in endless agitation. As the early reviews attested, the shock of finding living characters in the final pages of *Ethan Frome* is far worse, for most readers, than hearing of dead ones: 'sometimes the two of them get going at each other, and then Ethan's face'd break your heart' (p. 114).

PAMELA KNIGHTS
University of Durham

A SELECTIVE BIBLIOGRAPHY

Elizabeth Ammons, *Edith Wharton's Argument with America*, University of Georgia Press, Athens 1980

Martha Banta, 'The Ghostly Gothic of Wharton's Everyday World', *American Literary Realism 1870–1910*, 27/1, Fall 1994, pp. 1–10

Kenneth Bernard, 'Imagery and Symbolism in *Ethan Frome*' (1961), *Readings on 'Ethan Frome'*, edited by Christopher Smith (details below)

Millicent Bell (ed.), *The Cambridge Companion to Edith Wharton* Cambridge University Press, New York 1996

Benstock, Shari, *No Gifts from Chance: A Biography of Edith Wharton*, Scribner's, New York 1994

Jean Frantz Blackall, 'Edith Wharton's Art of Ellipsis', *Journal of Narrative Technique*, 17, Spring 1987, pp. 145–62

John L. Brooke, *The Heart of the Commonwealth: Society and Political Culture in Worcester County, Massachusetts, 1713–1816*, Cambridge University Press, Cambridge 1989

Donna M. Campbell, 'Edith Wharton and the "Authoresses": The Critique of Local Color in Wharton's Early Fiction', *Studies in American Fiction*, 222/2, 1994, pp. 169–83

Donna M. Campbell, 'Rewriting the "Rose and Lavender Pages": *Ethan Frome* and Women's Local Color Fiction', *Speaking the Other Self: American Women Writers*, edited by Jeanne Campbell Reesman, University of Georgia Press, Athens 1997, pp. 263–77

Christopher Clark, *The Roots of Rural Capitalism: Western Massachusetts, 1780–1860*, Cornell University Press, Ithaca and London 1990

Theresa Craig, *Edith Wharton: A House Full of Rooms: Architecture, Interiors, and Gardens*, Monacelli Press, New York 1996

Eleanor Dwight, *Edith Wharton: An Extraordinary Life*, Harry N. Abrams, New York 1994

The Edith Wharton Society website at http://www.gonzaga. edu/faculty/campbell/wharton/index/html (a wonderfully rich site, which includes bibliographies, on-line reviews and many links)

Julia Ehrhardt, *Edith Wharton and Her Novels*, BBC Educational Developments, London 1995 (a video and audio-cassette study pack for students, with discussion and criticism of novels and films by leading Wharton scholars)

Gloria C. Erlich, *The Sexual Education of Edith Wharton*, University of California Press, Berkeley 1992

Maria Magdalena Farland, '*Ethan Frome* and the "Springs" of Masculinity', *Modern Fiction Studies*, 42/4, 1996, pp. 707–29

Kathy A. Fedorko, *Gender and the Gothic in the Fiction of Edith Wharton*, University of Alabama Press, Tuscaloosa 1995

Robert Frost, *The Complete Poems of Robert Frost*, Jonathan Cape, London 1951

Judith Fryer, *Felicitous Space. The Imaginative Structures of Edith Wharton and Willa Cather*, University of North Carolina Press, Chapel Hill 1986

Stella Gibbons, *Cold Comfort Farm*, Longmans & Co, London 1932

Janet Beer Goodwyn, *Edith Wharton: Traveller in the Land of Letters*, Basingstoke, Macmillan 1990

Kate Gschwend, 'The Significance of the Sawmill: Technological Determinism in *Ethan Frome*', *Edith Wharton Review*, 16/1, Spring 2000, pp. 9–13

Wm Thomas Hill, '"Man-Like, He Sought to Postpone Certainty": Shadows of Truth and Identity in Edith Wharton's *Ethan Frome*', *Studies in the Humanities*, 56, 1995, pp. 63–82

Henry James, Preface to 'The Author of Beltraffio', in *French Writers, Other European Writers, The Prefaces to the New York Edition*, The Library of America, New York 1984, pp. 1238–45

Wook-Dong Kim, 'Theme and Symbol in Wharton's *Ethan Frome*', *Journal of English Language and Literature*, Winter 1989, pp. 677–94

Kristin Lauer and Margaret Murray (eds), *Edith Wharton: A Bibliography*, Garland, New York 1989

R. W. B Lewis, *Edith Wharton: A Biography*, Harper & Row, New York 1975

R. W. B. Lewis and Nancy Lewis (eds), *The Letters of Edith Wharton*, Scribners, New York 1989

R. W. B. Lewis (ed.), *Edith Wharton: Novels*, The Library of America, New York 1985

W. D. MacCallan, 'The French Draft of *Ethan Frome*', *Yale University Library Gazette*, 27/1, July 1953, pp. 38–47

Scott Marshall, 'Edith Wharton, Kate Spencer, and *Ethan Frome*', *Edith Wharton Review*, 10/1, 1993, pp. 20–1

Margaret McDowell, *Edith Wharton*, Twayne, Boston 1972; revised second edition, 1991

The Mount: Edith Wharton Restoration, website at http://www.edithwharton.org/

James F. Muirhead (ed.), *The United States. A Handbook for Travellers*, Karl Baedeker, Leipzig and New York 1893

Elsa Nettels, 'Gender and First-Person Narration in Edith Wharton's Short Fiction', *Edith Wharton: New Critical Essays*, edited by Alfred Bendixen and Annette Zilversmit, Garland, New York and London 1992, pp. 245–60

David E. Nye, *Electrifying America: Social Meanings of a New Technology*, Massachusetts Institute of Technology Press, Cambridge, Massachusetts 1990

Katherine Anne Porter, *The Collected Stories*, Virago, London 1985

Lyall H. Powers (ed.), *Henry James and Edith Wharton: Letters: 1900–1915*, Charles Scribner's and Macmillan, New York 1990

Thomas Schlereth, 'Country Stores, County Fairs, and Mail-Order Catalogues: Consumption in Rural America', *Consuming Visions: Accumulation and Display of Goods in America, 1880–1920*, edited by Simon J. Bronner, W.W. Norton, New York 1989, pp. 339–75

Elizabeth Shepley Sergeant, *New Republic*, 3, 8 May 1915, pp. 20–1

Carol J. Singley, *Edith Wharton: Matters of Mind and Spirit*, Cambridge University Press, Cambridge and New York 1995

Christopher Smith (ed.), *Readings on 'Ethan Frome'*, Greenhaven Press, San Diego, California 2000 (a useful anthology of essays exemplifying various critical approaches)

Marlene Springer, *'Ethan Frome': A Nightmare of Need*, Twayne, New York 1993

Jenniver Travis, 'Pain and Recompense: The Trouble with *Ethan Frome*', *Arizona Quarterly*, 53/3, Autumn 1997, pp. 37–64

James Tuttleton, Kristin Lauer and Margaret P. Murray (eds), *Edith Wharton: The Contemporary Reviews*, Garland, New York 1992

Candace Waid, *Edith Wharton's Letters from the Underworld: Fictions of Women and Writing*, University of North Carolina Press, Chapel Hill 1991

Edith Wharton, *A Backward Glance*, D. Appleton-Century Company, New York and London 1934

Edith Wharton, *The Uncollected Critical Writings*, edited by Frederick Wegener, Princeton University Press, Princeton, New Jersey 1996 (for Wharton's commentaries on *Ethan Frome*)

Cynthia Griffin Wolff, *The Triumph of Edith Wharton: A Feast of Words*, Addison-Wesley, New York 1977, 1995

Sarah Bird Wright, *Edith Wharton A to Z*, Checkmark Books, Facts on File, New York 1998 (an excellent illustrated starting-point and guide, containing details of screen and theatre adaptations, as well as information on Wharton's life and works, and critical treatment)

AUTHOR'S INTRODUCTION

I HAD KNOWN SOMETHING of New England village life long before I made my home in the same county as my imaginary Starkfield;[1] though, during the years spent there, certain of its aspects became much more familiar to me.

Even before that final initiation, however, I had had an uneasy sense that the New England of fiction[2] bore little – except a vague botanical and dialectical – resemblance to the harsh and beautiful land as I had seen it. Even the abundant enumeration of sweet-fern, asters and mountain-laurel, and the conscientious reproduction of the vernacular, left me with the feeling that the outcropping granite had in both cases been overlooked. I give the impression merely as a personal one; it accounts for *Ethan Frome*, and may, to some readers, in a measure justify it.

So much for the origin of the story; there is nothing else of interest to say of it, except as concerns its construction.

The problem before me, as I saw in the first flash, was this: I had to deal with a subject of which the dramatic climax, or rather the anti-climax, occurs a generation later than the first acts of the tragedy. This enforced lapse of time would seem to anyone persuaded – as I have always been – that every subject (in the novelist's sense of the term) implicitly *contains its own form and dimensions*, to mark 'Ethan Frome' as the subject of a novel. But I never thought this for a moment, for I had felt, at the same time, that the theme of my tale was not one on which many variations could be played. It must be treated as starkly and summarily as life had always presented itself to my protagonists; any attempt to elaborate and complicate their sentiments would necessarily have falsified the whole. They were, in truth, these figures, my *granite outcroppings*; but half emerged from the soil, and scarcely more articulate.

This incompatibility between subject and plan would perhaps have seemed to suggest that my 'situation' was after all one to be rejected. Every novelist has been visited by the insinuating wraiths of false 'good situations', siren-subjects luring his cockle-shell to the rocks; their voice is oftenest heard, and their mirage-sea beheld, as he traverses the waterless desert which awaits him half-way through whatever work is actually in hand. I knew well enough what song those sirens sang, and had often tied myself to my dull job till they were out of hearing – perhaps carrying a lost masterpiece in their rainbow veils. But I had no such fear of them in the case of *Ethan Frome*. It was the first subject I had ever approached with full confidence in its value, for my own purpose, and a relative faith in my power to render at least a part of what I saw in it.

Every novelist, again, who 'intends upon' his art, has lit upon such subjects, and been fascinated by the difficulty of presenting them in the fullest relief, yet without an added ornament or a trick of drapery or lighting. This was my task, if I were to tell the story of Ethan Frome; and my scheme of construction – which met with the immediate and unqualified disapproval of the few friends to whom I tentatively outlined it – I still think justified in the given case. It appears to me, indeed, that, while an air of artificiality is lent to a tale of complex and sophisticated people which the novelist causes to be guessed at and interpreted by any mere onlooker, there need be no such drawback if the looker-on is sophisticated, and the people he interprets are simple. If he is capable of seeing all around them, no violence is done to probability in allowing him to exercise this faculty; it is natural enough that he should act as the sympa-thising intermediary between his rudimentary characters and the more complicated minds to whom he is trying to present them. But this is all self-evident, and needs explaining only to those who have never thought of fiction as an art of composition.

The real merit of my construction seems to me to lie in a minor detail. I had to find means to bring my tragedy, in a way at once natural and picture-making, to the knowledge of its narrator. I might have sat him down before a village gossip who would have poured out the whole affair to him in a breath, but in doing this I should have been false to two essential elements of my picture: first, the deep-rooted reticence and inarticulateness of the people I was trying to draw, and secondly the effect of 'roundness' (in the plastic sense) produced by letting their case be seen through eyes as different as those of Harmon Gow and Mrs Ned Hale. Each of my chroniclers contributes to the narrative *just so much as he or she is capable of understanding* of what, to them, is a complicated and mysterious case;

and only the narrator of the tale has scope enough to see it all, to resolve it back into simplicity, and to put it in its rightful place among his larger categories.

I make no claim for originality in following a method of which *La Grande Bretêche*[3] and *The Ring and the Book*[4] had set me the magnificent example; my one merit is, perhaps, to have guessed that the proceeding there employed was also applicable to my small tale.

I have written this brief analysis – the first I have ever published of any of my books – because, as an author's introduction to his work, I can imagine nothing of any value to his readers except a statement as to why he decided to attempt the work in question, and why he selected one form rather than another for its embodiment. These primary aims, the only ones that can be explicitly stated, must, by the artist, be almost instinctively felt and acted upon before there can pass into his creation that imponderable something more which causes life to circulate in it, and preserves it for a little from decay.

EDITH WHARTON
31 March 1922

I HAD THE STORY, bit by bit, from various people, and, as generally happens in such cases, each time it was a different story.

If you know Starkfield, Massachusetts, you know the post-office. If you know the post-office you must have seen Ethan Frome drive up to it, drop the reins on his hollow-backed bay and drag himself across the brick pavement to the white colonnade: and you must have asked who he was.

It was there that, several years ago, I saw him for the first time; and the sight pulled me up sharp. Even then he was the most striking figure in Starkfield, though he was but the ruin of a man. It was not so much his great height that marked him, for the 'natives' were easily singled out by their lank longitude from the stockier foreign breed: it was the careless powerful look he had, in spite of a lameness checking each step like the jerk of a chain. There was something bleak and unapproachable in his face, and he was so stiffened and grizzled that I took him for an old man and was surprised to hear that he was not more than fifty-two. I had this from Harmon Gow, who had driven the stage from Bettsbridge to Starkfield in pre-trolley[5] days and knew the chronicle of all the families on his line.

'He's looked that way ever since he had his smash-up; and that's twenty-four years ago come next February,' Harmon threw out between reminiscent pauses.

The 'smash-up' it was – I gathered from the same informant – which, besides drawing the red gash across Ethan Frome's forehead, had so shortened and warped his right side that it cost him a visible effort to take the few steps from his buggy to the post-office window. He used to drive in from his farm every day at about noon, and as that was my own hour for fetching my mail I often passed him in the porch or stood beside him while we waited on the motions of the distributing hand behind the grating. I noticed that, though he came so punctually, he seldom received anything but a copy of the *Bettsbridge Eagle*, which he put without a glance into his sagging pocket. At intervals, however, the postmaster would hand him an envelope addressed to Mrs Zenobia – or Mrs Zeena – Frome, and usually bearing conspicuously in the upper left-hand corner the address of some manufacturer of patent medicine and the name of his specific.[6] These documents my neighbour would also pocket without a glance, as if too much used to them to wonder at their number and variety, and would then turn away with a silent nod to the postmaster.

Everyone in Starkfield knew him and gave him a greeting tempered to his own grave mien; but his taciturnity was respected and it was only on rare occasions that one of the older men of the place detained him for a word. When this happened he would listen quietly, his blue eyes on the speaker's face, and answer in so low a tone that his words never reached me; then he would climb stiffly into his buggy, gather up the reins in his left hand and drive slowly away in the direction of his farm.

'It was a pretty bad smash-up?' I questioned Harmon, looking after Frome's retreating figure, and thinking how gallantly his lean brown head, with its shock of light hair, must have sat on his strong shoulders before they were bent out of shape.

'Wust kind,' my informant assented. 'More'n enough to kill most men. But the Fromes are tough. Ethan'll likely touch a hundred.'

'Good God!' I exclaimed. At that moment Ethan Frome, after climbing to his seat, had leaned over to assure himself of the security of a wooden box – also with a druggist's label on it – which he had placed in the back of the buggy, and I saw his face as it probably looked when he thought himself alone. '*That* man touch a hundred? He looks as if he was dead and in hell now!'

Harmon drew a slab of tobacco from his pocket, cut off a wedge and pressed it into the leather pouch of his cheek. 'Guess he's been in Starkfield too many winters. Most of the smart ones get away.'

'Why didn't *he*?'

'Somebody had to stay and care for the folks. There warn't ever anybody but Ethan. Fust his father – then his mother – then his wife.'

'And then the smash-up?'

Harmon chuckled sardonically. 'That's so. He *had* to stay then.'

'I see. And since then they've had to care for him?'

Harmon thoughtfully passed his tobacco to the other cheek. 'Oh, as to that: I guess it's always Ethan done the caring.'

Though Harmon Gow developed the tale as far as his mental and moral reach permitted, there were perceptible gaps between his facts, and I had the sense that the deeper meaning of the story was in the gaps. But one phrase stuck in my memory and served as the nucleus about which I grouped my subsequent inferences: 'Guess he's been in Starkfield too many winters.'

Before my own time there was up I had learned to know what that meant. Yet I had come in the degenerate day of trolley, bicycle and rural delivery,[7] when communication was easy between the scattered mountain villages, and the bigger towns in the valleys, such as Bettsbridge and Shadd's Falls, had libraries, theatres and YMCA halls[8] to which the youth of the hills could descend for recreation. But when winter shut down on Starkfield, and the village lay under a sheet of snow perpetually renewed from the pale skies, I began to see what life there – or rather its negation – must have been in Ethan Frome's young manhood.

I had been sent up by my employers on a job connected with the big power-house[9] at Corbury Junction, and a long-drawn-out carpenters' strike had so delayed the work that I found myself anchored at Starkfield – the nearest habitable spot – for the best part of the winter. I chafed at first, and then, under the hypnotising effect of routine, gradually began to find a grim satisfaction in the life. During the early part of my stay I had been struck by the contrast between the vitality of the climate and the deadness of the community. Day by day, after the December snows were over, a blazing blue sky poured down torrents of light and air on the white landscape, which gave them back in an intenser glitter. One would have supposed that such an atmosphere must quicken the emotions as well as the blood; but it seemed to produce no change except that of retarding still more the sluggish pulse of Starkfield. When I had been there a little longer, and had seen this phase of crystal clearness followed by long stretches of sunless cold; when the storms of February had pitched their white tents about the devoted village and the wild cavalry of March winds had charged down to their support; I began to understand why Starkfield emerged from its six months' siege like a starved garrison capitulating without quarter. Twenty years earlier the means of resistance must have been far fewer, and the enemy in command of almost all the lines of access between the beleaguered villages; and, considering these things, I felt the sinister force of Harmon's phrase: 'Most of the smart ones get away.' But if that were the case, how could any combination of obstacles have hindered the flight of a man like Ethan Frome?

During my stay at Starkfield I lodged with a middle-aged widow colloquially known as Mrs Ned Hale. Mrs Hale's father had been the village lawyer of the previous generation, and 'lawyer Varnum's house', where my landlady still lived with her mother, was the most considerable mansion in the village. It stood at one end of the main street, its classic portico and small-paned windows looking down a flagged path between Norway spruces to the slim white steeple of the Congregational church. It was clear that the Varnum fortunes were at the ebb, but the two women did what they could to preserve a decent dignity; and Mrs Hale, in particular, had a certain wan refinement not out of keeping with her pale old-fashioned house.

In the 'best parlour', with its black horsehair and mahogany weakly illuminated by a gurgling Carcel lamp,[10] I listened every evening to another and more delicately shaded version of the Starkfield chronicle. It was not that Mrs Ned Hale felt, or affected, any social superiority to the people about her; it was only that the accident of a finer sensibility and a little more education had put just enough distance between herself and her neighbours to enable her to judge them with detachment. She was not unwilling to exercise this faculty, and I had great hopes of getting from her the missing facts of Ethan Frome's story, or rather such a key to his character as should co-ordinate the facts I knew. Her mind was a store-house of innocuous anecdote and any question about her acquaintances brought forth a volume of detail; but on the subject of Ethan Frome I found her unexpectedly reticent. There was no hint of disapproval in her reserve; I merely felt in her an insurmountable reluctance to speak of him or his affairs, a low 'Yes, I knew them both . . . it was awful . . . ' seeming to be the utmost concession that her distress could make to my curiosity.

So marked was the change in her manner, such depths of sad initiation did it imply, that, with some doubts as to my delicacy, I put the case anew to my village oracle, Harmon Gow; but got for my pains only an uncomprehending grunt.

'Ruth Varnum was always as nervous as a rat; and, come to think of it, she was the first one to see 'em after they was picked up. It happened right below lawyer Varnum's, down at the bend of the Corbury road, just round about the time that Ruth got engaged to Ned Hale. The young folks was all friends, and I guess she just can't bear to talk about it. She's had troubles enough of her own.'

All the dwellers in Starkfield, as in more notable communities, had had troubles enough of their own to make them comparatively indifferent to those of their neighbours; and though all conceded that Ethan Frome's had been beyond the common measure, no one gave me an explanation of the look in his face which, as I persisted in thinking, neither poverty nor physical suffering could have put there. Nevertheless, I might have contented myself with the story pieced together from these hints had it not been for the provocation of Mrs Hale's silence, and – a little later – for the accident of personal contact with the man.

On my arrival at Starkfield, Denis Eady, the rich Irish grocer, who was the proprietor of Starkfield's nearest approach to a livery stable, had entered into an agreement to send me over daily to Corbury Flats, where I had to pick up my train for the Junction. But about the middle of the winter Eady's horses fell ill of a local epidemic. The illness spread to the other Starkfield stables and for a day or two I was put to it to find a means of transport. Then Harmon Gow suggested that Ethan Frome's bay was still on his legs and that his owner might be glad to drive me over.

I stared at the suggestion. 'Ethan Frome? But I've never even spoken to him. Why on earth should he put himself out for me?'

Harmon's answer surprised me still more. 'I don't know as he would; but I know he wouldn't be sorry to earn a dollar.'

I had been told that Frome was poor, and that the sawmill and the arid acres of his farm yielded scarcely enough to keep his household through the winter; but I had not supposed him to be in such want as Harmon's words implied, and I expressed my wonder.

'Well, matters ain't gone any too well with him,' Harmon said. 'When a man's been setting round like a hulk for twenty years or more, seeing things that want doing, it eats inter him, and he loses his grit. That Frome farm was always 'bout as bare's a milkpan when the cat's been round; and you know what one of them old water-mills is wuth nowadays. When Ethan could sweat over 'em both from sun-up to dark he kinder choked a living out of 'em; but his folks ate up most everything, even then, and I don't see how he makes out now. Fust his father got a kick, out haying, and went soft in the brain, and gave away money like Bible texts afore he died. Then his mother got queer and dragged along for years as weak as a baby; and his wife Zeena, she's always been the greatest hand at doctoring in the county. Sickness and trouble: that's what Ethan's had his plate full up with, ever since the very first helping.'

The next morning, when I looked out, I saw the hollow-backed bay between the Varnum spruces, and Ethan Frome, throwing back his worn bearskin, made room for me in the sleigh at his side. After that, for a week, he drove me over every morning to Corbury Flats, and on my return in the afternoon met me again and carried me back through the icy night to Starkfield. The distance each way was barely three miles, but the old bay's pace was slow, and even with firm snow under the runners we were nearly an hour on the way. Ethan Frome drove in silence, the reins loosely held in his left hand, his brown seamed profile, under the helmet-like peak of the cap, relieved against the banks of snow like the bronze image of a hero. He never turned his face to mine, or answered, except in mono-syllables, the questions I put, or such slight pleasantries as I ventured. He seemed a part of the mute melancholy landscape, an incarnation of its frozen woe, with all that was warm and sentient in him fast bound below the surface; but there was nothing unfriendly in his silence. I simply felt that he lived in a depth of moral isolation too remote for casual access, and I had the sense that his loneliness was not merely the result of his personal plight, tragic as I guessed that to be, but had in it, as Harmon Gow had hinted, the profound accumulated cold of many Starkfield winters.

Only once or twice was the distance between us bridged for a moment; and the glimpses thus gained confirmed my desire to know more. Once I happened to speak of an engineering job I had been on the previous year in Florida, and of the contrast between the winter landscape about us and that in which I had found myself the year before; and to my surprise Frome said suddenly: 'Yes: I was down there once, and for a good while afterward I could call up the sight of it in winter. But now it's all snowed under.'

He said no more, and I had to guess the rest from the inflection of his voice and his sharp relapse into silence.

Another day, on getting into my train at the Flats, I missed a volume of popular science – I think it was on some recent discoveries in biochemistry – which I had carried with me to read on the way. I thought no more about it till I got into the sleigh again that evening, and saw the book in Frome's hand.

'I found it after you were gone,' he said.

I put the volume into my pocket and we dropped back into our usual silence; but as we began to crawl up the long hill from Corbury Flats to the Starkfield ridge I became aware in the dusk that he had turned his face to mine.

'There are things in that book that I didn't know the first word about,' he said.

I wondered less at his words than at the queer note of resentment in his voice. He was evidently surprised and slightly aggrieved at his own ignorance.

'Does that sort of thing interest you?' I asked.

'It used to.'

'There are one or two rather new things in the book: there have been some big strides lately in that particular line of research.' I waited a moment for an answer that did not come; then I said: 'If you'd like to look the book through I'd be glad to leave it with you.'

He hesitated, and I had the impression that he felt himself about to yield to a stealing tide of inertia; then, 'Thank you – I'll take it,' he answered shortly.

I hoped that this incident might set up some more direct communication between us. Frome was so simple and straightforward that I was sure his curiosity about the book was based on a genuine interest in its subject. Such tastes and acquirements in a man of his condition made the contrast more poignant between his outer situation and his inner needs, and I hoped that the chance of giving expression to the latter might at least unseal his lips. But something in his past history, or in his present way of living, had apparently driven him too deeply into himself for any casual impulse to draw him back to his kind. At our next meeting he made no allusion to the book, and our intercourse seemed fated to remain as negative and one-sided as if there had been no break in his reserve.

Frome had been driving me over to the Flats for about a week when one morning I looked out of my window into a thick snowfall. The height of the white waves massed against the garden fence and along the wall of the church showed that the storm must have been going on all night, and that the drifts were likely to be heavy in the open. I thought it probable that my train would be delayed; but I had to be at the power-house for an hour or two that afternoon, and I decided, if Frome turned up, to push through to the Flats and wait there till my train came in. I don't know why I put it in the conditional, however, for I never doubted that Frome would appear. He was not the kind of man to be turned from his business by any commotion of the elements; and at the appointed hour his sleigh glided up through the snow like a stage-apparition behind thickening veils of gauze.

I was getting to know him too well to express either wonder or gratitude at his keeping his appointment; but I exclaimed in surprise as I saw him turn his horse in a direction opposite to that of the Corbury road.

'The railroad's blocked by a freight-train that got stuck in a drift below the Flats,' he explained, as we jogged off into the stinging whiteness.

'But look here – where are you taking me, then?'

'Straight to the Junction, by the shortest way,' he answered, pointing up School House Hill with his whip.

'To the Junction – in this storm? Why, it's a good ten miles!'

'The bay'll do it if you give him time. You said you had some business there this afternoon. I'll see you get there.'

He said it so quietly that I could only answer: 'You're doing me the biggest kind of a favour.'

'That's all right,' he rejoined.

Abreast of the schoolhouse the road forked, and we dipped down a lane to the left, between hemlock boughs bent inward to their trunks by the weight of the snow. I had often walked that way on Sundays, and I knew that the solitary roof showing through bare branches near the bottom of the hill was that of Frome's sawmill. It looked exanimate enough, with its idle wheel looming above the black stream dashed with yellow-white spume, and its cluster of sheds sagging under their white load. Frome did not even turn his head as we drove by, and still in silence we began to mount the next slope. About a mile farther on, a road I had never travelled, we came to an orchard of starved apple trees writhing over a hillside among outcroppings of slate that nuzzled up through the snow like animals pushing out their noses to breathe. Beyond the orchard lay a field or two, their boundaries lost under drifts; and above the fields, huddled against the white immensities of land and sky, one of those lonely New England farmhouses that make the landscape lonelier.

'That's my place,' said Frome, with a sideway jerk of his lame elbow; and in the distress and oppression of the scene I did not know what to answer. The snow had ceased, and a flash of watery sunlight exposed the house on the slope above us in all its plaintive ugliness. The black wraith of a deciduous creeper flapped from the porch, and the thin wooden walls, under their worn coat of paint, seemed to shiver in the wind that had risen with the ceasing of the snow.

'The house was bigger in my father's time: I had to take down the L, a while back,' Frome continued, checking with a twitch of the left rein the bay's evident intention of turning in through the broken-down gate.

I saw then that the unusually forlorn and stunted look of the house was partly due to the loss of what is known in New England as the 'L': that long deep-roofed adjunct usually built at right angles to the main house, and connecting it, by way of store-rooms and tool-house, with the woodshed and cow-barn. Whether because of its symbolic sense, the image it presents of a life linked with the soil, and enclosing in itself the chief sources of warmth and nourishment, or whether merely because of the consolatory thought that it enables the dwellers in that harsh climate to get to their morning's work without facing the weather, it is certain that the L rather than the house itself seems to be the centre, the actual hearthstone of the New England farm. Perhaps this connection of ideas, which had often occurred to me in my rambles about Starkfield, caused me to hear a wistful note in Frome's words, and to see in the diminished dwelling the image of his own shrunken body.

'We're kinder side-tracked here now,' he added, 'but there was considerable passing before the railroad was carried through to the Flats.' He roused the lagging bay with another twitch; then, as if the mere sight of the house had let me too deeply into his confidence for any further pretence of reserve, he went on slowly: 'I've always set down the worst of mother's trouble to that. When she got the rheumatism so bad she couldn't move around she used to sit up there and watch the road by the hour; and one year, when they was six months mending the Bettsbridge pike after the floods, and Harmon Gow had to bring his stage round this way, she picked up so that she used to get down to the gate most days to see him. But after the trains begun running nobody ever come by here to speak of, and mother never could get it through her head what had happened, and it preyed on her right along till she died.'

As we turned into the Corbury road the snow began to fall again, cutting off our last glimpse of the house; and Frome's silence fell with it, letting down between us the old veil of reticence. This time the wind did not cease with the return of the snow. Instead, it sprang up to a gale which now and then, from a tattered sky, flung pale sweeps of sunlight over a landscape chaotically tossed. But the bay was as good as Frome's word, and we pushed on to the Junction through the wild white scene.

In the afternoon the storm held off, and the clearness in the west seemed to my inexperienced eye the pledge of a fair evening. I finished my business as quickly as possible, and we set out for Starkfield with a good chance of getting there for supper. But at sunset the clouds gathered again, bringing an earlier night, and the snow began to fall straight and steadily from a sky without wind, in a soft universal diffusion more confusing than the gusts and eddies of the morning. It seemed to be a part of the thickening darkness, to be the winter night itself descending on us layer by layer.

The small ray of Frome's lantern was soon lost in this smothering medium, in which even his sense of direction, and the bay's homing instinct, finally ceased to serve us. Two or three times some ghostly landmark sprang up to warn us that we were astray, and then was sucked back into the mist; and when we finally regained our road the old horse began to show signs of exhaustion. I felt myself to blame for having accepted Frome's offer, and after a short discussion I persuaded him to let me get out of the sleigh and walk along through the snow at the bay's side. In this way we struggled on for another mile or two, and at last reached a point where Frome, peering into what seemed to me formless night, said: 'That's my gate down yonder.'

The last stretch had been the hardest part of the way. The bitter cold and the heavy going had nearly knocked the wind out of me, and I could feel the horse's side ticking like a clock under my hand.

'Look here, Frome,' I began, 'there's no earthly use in your going any farther – ' but he interrupted me: 'Nor you neither. There's been about enough of this for anybody.'

I understood that he was offering me a night's shelter at the farm, and without answering I turned into the gate at his side, and followed him to the barn, where I helped him to unharness and bed down the tired horse. When this was done he unhooked the lantern from the sleigh, stepped out again into the night, and called to me over his shoulder: 'This way.'

Far off above us a square of light trembled through the screen of snow. Staggering along in Frome's wake I floundered toward it, and in the darkness almost fell into one of the deep drifts against the front of the house. Frome scrambled up the slippery steps of the porch, digging a way through the snow with his heavily booted foot. Then he lifted his lantern, found the latch, and led the way into the house. I went after him into a low unlit passage, at the back of which a ladder-like staircase rose into obscurity. On our right a line of light marked the door of the room which had sent its ray across the night; and behind the door I heard a woman's voice droning querulously.

Frome stamped on the worn oilcloth to shake the snow from his boots, and set down his lantern on a kitchen chair which was the only piece of furniture in the hall. Then he opened the door.

'Come in,' he said; and as he spoke the droning voice grew still . . .

It was that night that I found the clue to Ethan Frome, and began to put together this vision of his story . . . .
. . . .
. . . .

CHAPTER ONE

THE VILLAGE lay under two feet of snow, with drifts at the windy corners. In a sky of iron the points of the Dipper hung like icicles and Orion[11] flashed his cold fires. The moon had set, but the night was so transparent that the white house-fronts between the elms looked grey against the snow, clumps of bushes made black stains on it, and the basement windows of the church sent shafts of yellow light far across the endless undulations.

Young Ethan Frome walked at a quick pace along the deserted street, past the bank and Michael Eady's new brick store and lawyer Varnum's house with the two black Norway spruces at the gate. Opposite the Varnum gate, where the road fell away toward the Corbury valley, the church reared its slim white steeple and narrow peristyle. As the young man walked toward it the upper windows drew a black arcade along the side wall of the building, but from the lower openings, on the side where the ground sloped steeply down to the Corbury road, the light shot its long bars, illuminating many fresh furrows in the track leading to the basement door, and showing, under an adjoining shed, a line of sleighs with heavily blanketed horses.

The night was perfectly still, and the air so dry and pure that it gave little sensation of cold. The effect produced on Frome was rather of a complete absence of atmosphere, as though nothing less tenuous than ether intervened between the white earth under his feet and the metallic dome overhead. 'It's like being in an exhausted receiver,'[12] he thought. Four or five years earlier he had taken a year's course at a technological college at Worcester,[13] and dabbled in the laboratory with a friendly professor of physics; and the images supplied by that experience still cropped up, at unexpected moments, through the totally different associations of thought in which he had since been living. His father's death, and the misfortunes following it, had put a premature end to Ethan's studies; but though they had not gone far enough to be of much practical use they had fed his fancy and made him aware of huge cloudy meanings behind the daily face of things.

As he strode along through the snow the sense of such meanings glowed in his brain and mingled with the bodily flush produced by his sharp tramp. At the end of the village he paused before the darkened front of the church. He stood there a moment, breathing quickly, and looking up and down the street, in which not another figure moved. The pitch of the Corbury road, below lawyer Varnum's spruces, was the favourite coasting-ground of Starkfield, and on clear evenings the church corner rang till late with the shouts of the coasters; but tonight not a sled darkened the whiteness of the long declivity. The hush of midnight lay on the village, and all its waking life was gathered behind the church windows, from which strains of dance-music flowed with the broad bands of yellow light.

The young man, skirting the side of the building, went down the slope toward the basement door. To keep out of range of the revealing rays from within he made a circuit through the untrodden snow and gradually approached the farther angle of the basement wall. Thence, still hugging the shadow, he edged his way cautiously forward to the nearest window, holding back his straight spare body and craning his neck till he got a glimpse of the room.

Seen thus, from the pure and frosty darkness in which he stood, it seemed to be seething in a mist of heat. The metal reflectors of the gas-jets sent crude waves of light against the whitewashed walls, and the iron flanks of the stove at the end of the hall looked as though they were heaving with volcanic fires. The floor was thronged with girls and young men. Down the side wall facing the window stood a row of kitchen chairs from which the older women had just risen. By this time the music had stopped, and the musicians – a fiddler, and the young lady who played the harmonium on Sundays – were hastily refreshing themselves at one corner of the supper table which aligned its devastated pie-dishes and ice-cream saucers on the platform at the end of the hall. The guests were preparing to leave, and the tide had already set toward the passage where coats and wraps were hung, when a young man with a sprightly foot and a shock of black hair shot into the middle of the floor and clapped his hands. The signal took instant effect. The musicians hurried to their instruments, the dancers – some already half-muffled for departure – fell into line down each side of the room, the older spectators slipped back to their chairs, and the lively young man, after diving about here and there in the throng, drew forth a girl who had already wound a cherry-coloured 'fascinator'[14] about her head, and, leading her up to the end of the floor, whirled her down its length to the bounding tune of a Virginia reel.

Frome's heart was beating fast. He had been straining for a glimpse of the dark head under the cherry-coloured scarf and it vexed him that another eye should have been quicker than his. The leader of the reel, who looked as if he had Irish blood in his veins, danced well, and his partner caught his fire. As she passed down the line, her light figure swinging from hand to hand in circles of increasing swiftness, the scarf flew off her head and stood out behind her shoulders, and Frome, at each turn, caught sight of her laughing panting lips, the cloud of dark hair about her forehead, and the dark eyes which seemed the only fixed points in a maze of flying lines.

The dancers were going faster and faster, and the musicians, to keep up with them, belaboured their instruments like jockeys lashing their mounts on the home stretch; yet it seemed to the young man at the window that the reel would never end. Now and then he turned his eyes from the girl's face to that of her partner, which, in the exhilaration of the dance, had taken on a look of almost impudent ownership. Denis Eady was the son of Michael Eady, the ambitious Irish grocer, whose suppleness and effrontery had given Starkfield its first notion of 'smart' business methods, and whose new brick store testified to the success of the attempt. His son seemed likely to follow in his steps, and was meanwhile applying the same arts to the conquest of the Starkfield maidenhood. Hitherto Ethan Frome had been content to think him a mean fellow; but now he positively invited a horse-whipping. It was strange that the girl did not seem aware of it: that she could lift her rapt face to her dancer's, and drop her hands into his, without appearing to feel the offence of his look and touch.

Frome was in the habit of walking into Starkfield to fetch home his wife's cousin, Mattie Silver, on the rare evenings when some chance of amusement drew her to the village. It was his wife who had suggested, when the girl came to live with them, that such opportunities should be put in her way. Mattie Silver came from Stamford, and when she entered the Fromes' household to act as her cousin Zeena's aid it was thought best, as she came without pay, not to let her feel too sharp a contrast between the life she had left and the isolation of a Starkfield farm. But for this – as Frome sardonically reflected – it would hardly have occurred to Zeena to take any thought for the girl's amusement.

When his wife first proposed that they should give Mattie an occasional evening out he had inwardly demurred at having to do the extra two miles to the village and back after his hard day on the farm; but not long afterward he had reached the point of wishing that Starkfield might give all its nights to revelry.

Mattie Silver had lived under his roof for a year, and from early morning till they met at supper he had frequent chances of seeing her; but no moments in her company were comparable to those when, her arm in his, and her light step flying to keep time with his long stride, they walked back through the night to the farm. He had taken to the girl from the first day, when he had driven over to the Flats to meet her, and she had smiled and waved to him from the train, crying out, 'You must be Ethan!' as she jumped down with her bundles, while he reflected, looking over her slight person: 'She don't look much on housework, but she ain't a fretter, anyhow.' But it was not only that the coming to his house of a bit of hopeful young life was like the lighting of a fire on a cold hearth. The girl was more than the bright serviceable creature he had thought her. She had an eye to see and an ear to hear: he could show her things and tell her things, and taste the bliss of feeling that all he imparted left long reverberations and echoes he could wake at will.

It was during their night walks back to the farm that he felt most intensely the sweetness of this communion. He had always been more sensitive than the people about him to the appeal of natural beauty. His unfinished studies had given form to this sensibility and even in his unhappiest moments field and sky spoke to him with a deep and powerful persuasion. But hitherto the emotion had remained in him as a silent ache, veiling with sadness the beauty that evoked it. He did not even know whether anyone else in the world felt as he did, or whether he was the sole victim of this mournful privilege. Then he learned that one other spirit had trembled with the same touch of wonder: that at his side, living under his roof and eating his bread, was a creature to whom he could say: 'That's Orion down yonder; the big fellow to the right is Aldebaran,[15] and the bunch of little ones – like bees swarming – they're the Pleiades[16] . . . ' or whom he could hold entranced before a ledge of granite thrusting up through the fern while he unrolled the huge panorama of the ice age, and the long dim stretches of succeeding time. The fact that admiration for his learning mingled with Mattie's wonder at what he taught was not the least part of his pleasure. And there were other sensations, less definable but more exquisite, which drew them together with a shock of silent joy: the cold red of sunset behind winter hills, the flight of cloud-flocks over slopes of golden stubble, or the intensely blue shadows of hemlocks on sunlit snow. When she said to him once: 'It looks just as if it was painted!' it seemed to Ethan that the art of definition could go no farther, and that words had at last been found to utter his secret soul . . .

As he stood in the darkness outside the church these memories came back with the poignancy of vanished things. Watching Mattie whirl down the floor from hand to hand he wondered how he could ever have thought that his dull talk interested her. To him, who was never gay but in her presence, her gaiety seemed plain proof of indifference. The face she lifted to her dancers was the same which, when she saw him, always looked like a window that has caught the sunset. He even noticed two or three gestures which, in his fatuity, he had thought she kept for him: a way of throwing her head back when she was amused, as if to taste her laugh before she let it out, and a trick of sinking her lids slowly when anything charmed or moved her.

The sight made him unhappy, and his unhappiness roused his latent fears. His wife had never shown any jealousy of Mattie, but of late she had grumbled increasingly over the housework and found oblique ways of attracting attention to the girl's inefficiency. Zeena had always been what Starkfield called 'sickly', and Frome had to admit that, if she were as ailing as she believed, she needed the help of a stronger arm than the one which lay so lightly in his during the night walks to the farm. Mattie had no natural turn for housekeeping, and her training had done nothing to remedy the defect. She was quick to learn, but forgetful and dreamy, and not disposed to take the matter seriously. Ethan had an idea that if she were to marry a man she was fond of the dormant instinct would wake, and her pies and biscuits become the pride of the county; but domesticity in the abstract did not interest her. At first she was so awkward that he could not help laughing at her; but she laughed with him and that made them better friends. He did his best to supplement her unskilled efforts, getting up earlier than usual to light the kitchen fire, carrying in the wood overnight, and neglecting the mill for the farm that he might help her about the house during the day. He even crept down on Saturday nights to scrub the kitchen floor after the women had gone to bed; and Zeena, one day, had surprised him at the churn and had turned away silently, with one of her queer looks.

Of late there had been other signs of her disfavour, as intangible but more disquieting. One cold winter morning, as he dressed in the dark, his candle flickering in the draught of the ill-fitting window, he had heard her speak from the bed behind him.

'The doctor don't want I should be left without anybody to do for me,' she said in her flat whine.

He had supposed her to be asleep, and the sound of her voice had startled him, though she was given to abrupt explosions of speech after long intervals of secretive silence.

He turned and looked at her where she lay indistinctly outlined under the dark calico quilt, her high-boned face taking a greyish tinge from the whiteness of the pillow.

'Nobody to do for you?' he repeated.

'If you say you can't afford a hired girl when Mattie goes.'

Frome turned away again, and taking up his razor stooped to catch the reflection of his stretched cheek in the blotched looking-glass above the washstand.

'Why on earth should Mattie go?'

'Well, when she gets married, I mean,' his wife's drawl came from behind him.

'Oh, she'd never leave us as long as you needed her,' he returned, scraping hard at his chin.

'I wouldn't ever have it said that I stood in the way of a poor girl like Mattie marrying a smart fellow like Denis Eady,' Zeena answered in a tone of plaintive self-effacement.

Ethan, glaring at his face in the glass, threw his head back to draw the razor from ear to chin. His hand was steady, but the attitude was an excuse for not making an immediate reply.

'And the doctor don't want I should be left without anybody,' Zeena continued. 'He wanted I should speak to you about a girl he's heard about, that might come – '

Ethan laid down the razor and straightened himself with a laugh.

'Denis Eady! If that's all, I guess there's no such hurry to look round for a girl.'

'Well, I'd like to talk to you about it,' said Zeena obstinately.

He was getting into his clothes in fumbling haste. 'All right. But I haven't got the time now; I'm late as it is,' he returned, holding his old silver turnip-watch[17] to the candle.

Zeena, apparently accepting this as final, lay watching him in silence while he pulled his braces over his shoulders and jerked his arms into his coat; but as he went toward the door she said, suddenly and incisively: 'I guess you're always late, now you shave every morning.'

That thrust had frightened him more than any vague insinuations about Denis Eady. It was a fact that since Mattie Silver's coming he had taken to shaving every day; but his wife always seemed to be asleep when he left her side in the winter darkness, and he had stupidly assumed that she would not notice any change in his appearance. Once or twice in the past he had been faintly disquieted by Zenobia's way of letting things happen without seeming to remark them, and then, weeks afterward, in a casual phrase, revealing that she had all along taken her notes and drawn her inferences. Of late, however, there had been no room in his thoughts for such vague apprehensions. Zeena herself, from an oppressive reality, had faded into an insubstantial shade. All his life was lived in the sight and sound of Mattie Silver, and he could no longer conceive of its being otherwise. But now, as he stood outside the church, and saw Mattie spinning down the floor with Denis Eady, a throng of disregarded hints and menaces wove their cloud about his brain . . .

CHAPTER TWO

As THE DANCERS poured out of the hall Frome, drawing back behind the projecting storm-door, watched the segregation of the grotesquely muffled groups, in which a moving lantern ray now and then lit up a face flushed with food and dancing. The villagers, being afoot, were the first to climb the slope to the main street, while the country neighbours packed themselves more slowly into the sleighs under the shed.

'Ain't you riding, Mattie?' a woman's voice called back from the throng about the shed, and Ethan's heart gave a jump. From where he stood he could not see the persons coming out of the hall till they had advanced a few steps beyond the wooden sides of the storm-door; but through its cracks he heard a clear voice answer: 'Mercy no! Not on such a night.'

She was there, then, close to him, only a thin board between. In another moment she would step forth into the night, and his eyes, accustomed to the obscurity, would discern her as clearly as though she stood in daylight. A wave of shyness pulled him back into the dark angle of the wall, and he stood there in silence instead of making his presence known to her. It had been one of the wonders of their intercourse that from the first, she, the quicker, finer, more expressive, instead of crushing him by the contrast, had given him something of her own ease and freedom; but now he felt as heavy and loutish as in his student days, when he had tried to 'jolly' the Worcester girls at a picnic.

He hung back, and she came out alone and paused within a few yards of him. She was almost the last to leave the hall, and she stood looking uncertainly about her as if wondering why he did not show himself. Then a man's figure approached, coming so close to her that under their formless wrappings they seemed merged in one dim outline.

'Gentleman friend gone back on you? Say, Matt, that's tough! No, I wouldn't be mean enough to tell the other girls. I ain't as low-down as that.' (How Frome hated his cheap banter!) 'But look a here, ain't it lucky I got the old man's cutter down there waiting for us?'

Frome heard the girl's voice, gaily incredulous: 'What on earth's your father's cutter doin' down there?'

'Why, waiting for me to take a ride. I got the roan colt too, I kinder knew I'd want to take a ride tonight,' Eady, in his triumph, tried to put a sentimental note into his bragging voice.

The girl seemed to waver, and Frome saw her twirl the end of her scarf irresolutely about her fingers. Not for the world would he have made a sign to her, though it seemed to him that his life hung on her next gesture.

'Hold on a minute while I unhitch the colt,' Denis called to her, springing toward the shed.

She stood perfectly still, looking after him, in an attitude of tranquil expectancy torturing to the hidden watcher. Frome noticed that she no longer turned her head from side to side, as though peering through the night for another figure. She let Denis Eady lead out the horse, climb into the cutter and fling back the bearskin to make room for her at his side; then, with a swift motion of flight, she turned about and darted up the slope toward the front of the church.

'Goodbye! Hope you'll have a lovely ride!' she called back to him over her shoulder.

Denis laughed, and gave the horse a cut that brought him quickly abreast of her retreating figure.

'Come along! Get in quick! It's as slippery as thunder on this turn,' he cried, leaning over to reach out a hand to her.

She laughed back at him: 'Good-night! I'm not getting in.'

By this time they had passed beyond Frome's earshot and he could only follow the shadowy pantomime of their silhouettes as they continued to move along the crest of the slope above him. He saw Eady, after a moment, jump from the cutter and go toward the girl with the reins over one arm. The other he tried to slip through hers; but she eluded him nimbly, and Frome's heart, which had swung out over a black void, trembled back to safety. A moment later he heard the jingle of departing sleigh bells and discerned a figure advancing alone toward the empty expanse of snow before the church.

In the black shade of the Varnum spruces he caught up with her and she turned with a quick 'Oh!'

'Think I'd forgotten you, Matt?' he asked with sheepish glee.

She answered seriously: 'I thought maybe you couldn't come back for me.'

'Couldn't? What on earth could stop me?'

'I knew Zeena wasn't feeling any too good today.'

'Oh, she's in bed long ago.' He paused, a question struggling in him. 'Then you meant to walk home all alone?'

'Oh, I ain't afraid!' she laughed.

They stood together in the gloom of the spruces, an empty world glimmering about them wide and grey under the stars. He brought his question out.

'If you thought I hadn't come, why didn't you ride back with Denis Eady?'

'Why, where *were* you? How did you know? I never saw you!'

Her wonder and his laughter ran together like spring rills in a thaw. Ethan had the sense of having done something arch and ingenious. To prolong the effect he groped for a dazzling phrase, and brought out, in a growl of rapture: 'Come along.'

He slipped an arm through hers, as Eady had done, and fancied it was faintly pressed against her side; but neither of them moved. It was so dark under the spruces that he could barely see the shape of her head beside his shoulder. He longed to stoop his cheek and rub it against her scarf. He would have liked to stand there with her all night in the blackness. She moved forward a step or two and then paused again above the dip of the Corbury road. Its icy slope, scored by innumerable runners, looked like a mirror scratched by travellers at an inn.

'There was a whole lot of them coasting before the moon set,' she said.

'Would you like to come in and coast with them some night?' he asked.

'Oh, *would* you, Ethan? It would be lovely!'

'We'll come tomorrow if there's a moon.'

She lingered, pressing closer to his side. 'Ned Hale and Ruth Varnum came just as *near* running into the big elm at the bottom. We were all sure they were killed.' Her shiver ran down his arm. 'Wouldn't it have been too awful? They're so happy!'

'Oh, Ned ain't much at steering. I guess I can take you down all right!' he said disdainfully.

He was aware that he was 'talking big', like Denis Eady; but his reaction of joy had unsteadied him, and the inflection with which she had said of the engaged couple 'They're so happy!' made the words sound as if she had been thinking of herself and him.

'The elm *is* dangerous, though. It ought to be cut down,' she insisted.

'Would you be afraid of it, with me?'

'I told you I ain't the kind to be afraid,' she tossed back, almost indifferently; and suddenly she began to walk on with a rapid step.

These alterations of mood were the despair and joy of Ethan

Frome. The motions of her mind were as incalculable as the flit of a bird in the branches. The fact that he had no right to show his feelings, and thus provoke the expression of hers, made him attach a fantastic importance to every change in her look and tone. Now he thought she understood him, and feared; now he was sure she did not, and despaired. Tonight the pressure of accumulated misgivings sent the scale drooping toward despair, and her indifference was the more chilling after the flush of joy into which she had plunged him by dismissing Denis Eady. He mounted School House Hill at her side and walked on in silence till they reached the lane leading to the sawmill; then the need of some definite assurance grew too strong for him.

'You'd have found me right off if you hadn't gone back to have that last reel with Denis,' he brought out awkwardly. He could not pronounce the name without a stiffening of the muscles of his throat.

'Why, Ethan, how could I tell you were there?'

'I suppose what folks say is true,' he jerked out at her, instead of answering.

She stopped short, and he felt, in the darkness, that her face was lifted quickly to his. 'Why, what do folks say?'

'It's natural enough you should be leaving us,' he floundered on, following his thought.

'Is that what they say?' she mocked back at him; then, with a sudden drop of her sweet treble: 'You mean that Zeena – ain't suited with me any more?' she faltered.

Their arms had slipped apart and they stood motionless, each seeking to distinguish the other's face.

'I know I ain't anything like as smart as I ought to be,' she went on, while he vainly struggled for expression. 'There's lots of things a hired girl could do that come awkward to me still – and I haven't got much strength in my arms. But if she'd only tell me I'd try. You know she hardly ever says anything, and sometimes I can see she ain't suited, and yet I don't know why.' She turned on him with a sudden flash of indignation. 'You'd ought to tell me, Ethan Frome – you'd ought to! Unless *you* want me to go too – '

Unless he wanted her to go too! The cry was balm to his raw wound. The iron heavens seemed to melt and rain down sweetness. Again he struggled for the all-expressive word, and again, his arm in hers, found only a deep, 'Come along.'

They walked on in silence through the blackness of the hemlock-shaded lane, where Ethan's sawmill gloomed through the night, and out again into the comparative clearness of the fields. On the farther side of the hemlock belt the open country rolled away before them grey and lonely under the stars. Sometimes their way led them under the shade of an overhanging bank or through the thin obscurity of a clump of leafless trees. Here and there a farmhouse stood far back among the fields, mute and cold as a gravestone. The night was so still that they heard the frozen snow crackle under their feet. The crash of a loaded branch falling far off in the woods reverberated like a musket-shot, and once a fox barked, and Mattie shrank closer to Ethan, and quickened her steps.

At length they sighted the group of larches at Ethan's gate, and as they drew near it the sense that the walk was over brought back his words.

'Then you don't want to leave us, Matt?'

He had to stoop his head to catch her stifled whisper: 'Where'd I go, if I did?'

The answer sent a pang through him but the tone suffused him with joy. He forgot what else he had meant to say and pressed her against him so closely that he seemed to feel her warmth in his veins.

'You ain't crying, are you, Matt?'

'No, of course I'm not,' she quavered.

They turned in at the gate and passed under the shaded knoll where, enclosed in a low fence, the Frome gravestones slanted at crazy angles through the snow. Ethan looked at them curiously. For years that quiet company had mocked his restlessness, his desire for change and freedom. 'We never got away – how should you?' seemed to be written on every headstone; and whenever he went in or out of his gate he thought with a shiver: 'I shall just go on living here till I join them.' But now all desire for change had vanished, and the sight of the little enclosure gave him a warm sense of continuance and stability.

'I guess we'll never let you go, Matt,' he whispered, as though even the dead, lovers once, must conspire with him to keep her; and brushing by the graves, he thought: 'We'll always go on living here together, and someday she'll lie there beside me.'

He let the vision possess him as they climbed the hill to the house. He was never so happy with her as when he abandoned himself to these dreams. Half-way up the slope Mattie stumbled against some unseen obstruction and clutched his sleeve to steady herself. The wave of warmth that went through him was like the prolongation of his vision. For the first time he stole his arm about her, and she did not resist. They walked on as if they were floating on a summer stream.

Zeena always went to bed as soon as she had had her supper, and the shutterless windows of the house were dark. A dead cucumber-vine dangled from the porch like the crepe streamer tied to the door for a death, and the thought flashed through Ethan's brain: 'If it was there for Zeena – ' Then he had a distinct sight of his wife lying in their bedroom asleep, her mouth slightly open, her false teeth in a tumbler by the bed . . .

They walked around to the back of the house, between the rigid gooseberry bushes. It was Zeena's habit, when they came back late from the village, to leave the key of the kitchen door under the mat. Ethan stood before the door, his head heavy with dreams, his arm still about Mattie. 'Matt – ' he began, not knowing what he meant to say.

She slipped out of his hold without speaking, and he stooped down and felt for the key.

'It's not there!' he said, straightening himself with a start.

They strained their eyes at each other through the icy darkness. Such a thing had never happened before.

'Maybe she's forgotten it,' Mattie said in a tremulous whisper; but both of them knew that it was not like Zeena to forget.

'It might have fallen off into the snow,' Mattie continued, after a pause during which they had stood intently listening.

'It must have been pushed off, then,' he rejoined in the same tone. Another wild thought tore through him. What if tramps had been there – what if . . .

Again he listened, fancying he heard a distant sound in the house; then he felt in his pocket for a match, and kneeling down, passed its light slowly over the rough edges of snow about the doorstep.

He was still kneeling when his eyes, on a level with the lower panel of the door, caught a faint ray beneath it. Who could be stirring in that silent house? He heard a step on the stairs, and again for an instant the thought of tramps tore through him. Then the door opened and he saw his wife.

Against the dark background of the kitchen she stood up tall and angular, one hand drawing a quilted counterpane to her flat breast, while the other held a lamp. The light, on a level with her chin, drew out of the darkness her puckered throat and the projecting wrist of the hand that clutched the quilt, and deepened fantastically the hollows and prominences of her high-boned face under its ring of crimping-pins.[18] To Ethan, still in the rosy haze of his hour with Mattie, the sight came with the intense precision of the last dream before waking. He felt as if he had never before known what his wife looked like.

She drew aside without speaking, and Mattie and Ethan passed
into the kitchen, which had the deadly chill of a vault after the dry
cold of the night.

'Guess you forgot about us, Zeena,' Ethan joked, stamping the
snow from his boots.

'No. I just felt so mean I couldn't sleep.'

Mattie came forward, unwinding her wraps, the colour of the
cherry scarf in her fresh lips and cheeks. 'I'm so sorry, Zeena! Isn't
there anything I can do?'

'No; there's nothing.' Zeena turned away from her. 'You might 'a'
shook off that snow outside,' she said to her husband.

She walked out of the kitchen ahead of them and pausing in the
hall raised the lamp at arm's length, as if to light them up the stairs.

Ethan paused also, affecting to fumble for the peg on which he
hung his coat and cap. The doors of the two bedrooms faced each
other across the narrow upper landing, and tonight it was peculiarly
repugnant to him that Mattie should see him follow Zeena.

'I guess I won't come up yet awhile,' he said, turning as if to go
back to the kitchen.

Zeena stopped short and looked at him. 'For the land's sake – what
you going to do down here?'

'I've got the mill accounts to go over.'

She continued to stare at him, the flame of the unshaded lamp
bringing out with microscopic cruelty the fretful lines of her face.

'At this time o' night? You'll ketch your death. The fire's out long
ago.'

Without answering he moved away toward the kitchen. As he did
so his glance crossed Mattie's and he fancied that a fugitive warning
gleamed through her lashes. The next moment they sank to her
flushed cheeks and she began to mount the stairs ahead of Zeena.

'That's so. It *is* powerful cold down here,' Ethan assented; and with
lowered head he went up in his wife's wake, and followed her across
the threshold of their room.

CHAPTER THREE

THERE WAS SOME hauling to be done at the lower end of the wood-lot, and Ethan was out early the next day.

The winter morning was as clear as crystal. The sunrise burned red in a pure sky, the shadows on the rim of the wood-lot were darkly blue, and beyond the white and scintillating fields patches of far-off forest hung like smoke.

It was in the early morning stillness, when his muscles were swinging to their familiar task and his lungs expanding with long draughts of mountain air, that Ethan did his clearest thinking. He and Zeena had not exchanged a word after the door of their room had closed on them. She had measured out some drops from a medicine bottle on a chair by the bed and, after swallowing them, and wrapping her head in a piece of yellow flannel, had lain down with her face turned away. Ethan undressed hurriedly and blew out the light so that he should not see her when he took his place at her side. As he lay there he could hear Mattie moving about in her room, and her candle, sending its small ray across the landing, drew a scarcely perceptible line of light under his door. He kept his eyes fixed on the light till it vanished. Then the room grew perfectly black, and not a sound was audible but Zeena's asthmatic breathing. Ethan felt confusedly that there were many things he ought to think about, but through his tingling veins and tired brain only one sensation throbbed: the warmth of Mattie's shoulder against his. Why had he not kissed her when he held her there? A few hours earlier he would not have asked himself the question. Even a few minutes earlier, when they had stood alone outside the house, he would not have dared to think of kissing her. But since he had seen her lips in the lamplight he felt that they were his.

Now, in the bright morning air, her face was still before him. It was part of the sun's red and of the pure glitter on the snow. How the girl had changed since she had come to Starkfield! He remembered what a colourless slip of a thing she had looked the day he had met her at the station. And all the first winter, how she had shivered with cold when the northerly gales shook the thin clapboards and the snow beat like hail against the loose-hung windows!

He had been afraid that she would hate the hard life, the cold and

loneliness; but not a sign of discontent escaped her. Zeena took the
view that Mattie was bound to make the best of Starkfield since she
hadn't any other place to go to; but this did not strike Ethan as
conclusive. Zeena, at any rate, did not apply the principle in her own
case.

He felt all the more sorry for the girl because misfortune had, in a
sense, indentured[19] her to them. Mattie Silver was the daughter of a
cousin of Zenobia Frome's, who had inflamed his clan with mingled
sentiments of envy and admiration by descending from the hills to
Connecticut, where he had married a Stamford girl and succeeded to
her father's thriving drug business. Unhappily Orin Silver, a man of
far-reaching aims, had died too soon to prove that the end justifies
the means. His accounts revealed merely what the means had been;
and these were such that it was fortunate for his wife and daughter
that his books were examined only after his impressive funeral. His
wife died of the disclosure, and Mattie, at twenty, was left alone to
make her way on the fifty dollars obtained from the sale of her piano.
For this purpose her equipment, though varied, was inadequate. She
could trim a hat, make molasses candy, recite 'Curfew shall not ring
tonight',[20] and play *The Lost Chord*[21] and a pot-pourri from *Carmen*.[22]
When she tried to extend the field of her activities in the direction of
stenography and bookkeeping her health broke down, and six months
on her feet behind the counter of a department store did not tend to
restore it. Her nearest relations had been induced to place their
savings in her father's hands, and though, after his death, they
ungrudgingly acquitted themselves of the Christian duty of returning
good for evil by giving his daughter all the advice at their disposal,
they could hardly be expected to supplement it by material aid. But
when Zenobia's doctor recommended her looking about for someone
to help her with the housework the clan instantly saw the chance of
exacting a compensation from Mattie. Zenobia, though doubtful of
the girl's efficiency, was tempted by the freedom to find fault without
much risk of losing her; and so Mattie came to Starkfield.

Zenobia's fault-finding was of the silent kind, but not the less
penetrating for that. During the first months Ethan alternately
burned with the desire to see Mattie defy her and trembled with fear
of the result. Then the situation grew less strained. The pure air, and
the long summer hours in the open, gave back life and elasticity to
Mattie, and Zeena, with more leisure to devote to her complex
ailments, grew less watchful of the girl's omissions; so that Ethan,
struggling on under the burden of his barren farm and failing
sawmill, could at least imagine that peace reigned in his house.

There was really, even now, no tangible evidence to the contrary; but since the previous night a vague dread had hung on his skyline. It was formed of Zeena's obstinate silence, of Mattie's sudden look of warning, of the memory of just such fleeting imperceptible signs as those which told him, on certain stainless mornings, that before night there would be rain.

His dread was so strong that, man-like, he sought to postpone certainty. The hauling was not over till midday, and as the lumber was to be delivered to Andrew Hale, the Starkfield builder, it was really easier for Ethan to send Jotham Powell, the hired man, back to the farm on foot, and drive the load down to the village himself. He had scrambled up on the logs, and was sitting astride of them, close over his shaggy greys, when, coming between him and their streaming necks, he had a vision of the warning look that Mattie had given him the night before.

'If there's going to be any trouble I want to be there,' was his vague reflection, as he threw to Jotham the unexpected order to unhitch the team and lead them back to the barn.

It was a slow trudge home through the heavy fields, and when the two men entered the kitchen Mattie was lifting the coffee from the stove and Zeena was already at the table. Her husband stopped short at sight of her. Instead of her usual calico wrapper and knitted shawl she wore her best dress of brown merino, and above her thin strands of hair, which still preserved the tight undulations of the crimping-pins, rose a hard perpendicular bonnet, as to which Ethan's clearest notion was that he had to pay five dollars for it at the Bettsbridge Emporium. On the floor beside her stood his old valise and a bandbox wrapped in newspapers.

'Why, where are you going, Zeena?' he exclaimed.

'I've got my shooting pains so bad that I'm going over to Bettsbridge to spend the night with Aunt Martha Pierce and see that new doctor,' she answered in a matter-of-fact tone, as if she had said she was going into the store-room to take a look at the preserves, or up to the attic to go over the blankets.

In spite of her sedentary habits such abrupt decisions were not without precedent in Zeena's history. Twice or thrice before she had suddenly packed Ethan's valise and started off to Bettsbridge, or even Springfield,[23] to seek the advice of some new doctor, and her husband had grown to dread these expeditions because of their cost. Zeena always came back laden with expensive remedies, and her last visit to Springfield had been commemorated by her paying twenty dollars for an electric battery[24] of which she had never been able to learn the use. But for the moment his sense of relief was so great as to preclude all other feelings. He had now no doubt that Zeena had spoken the truth in saying, the night before, that she had sat up because she felt 'too mean' to sleep: her abrupt resolve to seek medical advice showed that, as usual, she was wholly absorbed in her health.

As if expecting a protest, she continued plaintively: 'If you're too busy with the hauling I presume you can let Jotham Powell drive me over with the sorrel in time to ketch the train at the Flats.'

Her husband hardly heard what she was saying. During the winter months there was no stage between Starkfield and Bettsbridge, and the trains which stopped at Corbury Flats were slow and infrequent. A rapid calculation showed Ethan that Zeena could not be back at the farm before the following evening . . .

'If I'd supposed you'd 'a' made any objection to Jotham Powell's driving me over – ' she began again, as though his silence had implied refusal. On the brink of departure she was always seized with a flux of words. 'All I know is,' she continued, 'I can't go on the way I am much longer. The pains are clear away down to my ankles now, or I'd 'a' walked in to Starkfield on my own feet, sooner'n put you out, and asked Michael Eady to let me ride over on his wagon to the Flats, when he sends to meet the train that brings his groceries. I'd 'a' had two hours to wait in the station, but I'd sooner 'a' done it, even with this cold, than to have you say – '

'Of course Jotham'll drive you over,' Ethan roused himself to answer. He became suddenly conscious that he was looking at Mattie while Zeena talked to him, and with an effort he turned his eyes to his wife. She sat opposite the window, and the pale light reflected from the banks of snow made her face look more than usually drawn and bloodless, sharpened the three parallel creases between ear and cheek, and drew querulous lines from her thin nose to the corners of her mouth. Though she was but seven years her husband's senior, and he was only twenty-eight, she was already an old woman.

Ethan tried to say something befitting the occasion, but there was only one thought in his mind: the fact that, for the first time since Mattie had come to live with them, Zeena was to be away for a night. He wondered if the girl were thinking of it too . . .

He knew that Zeena must be wondering why he did not offer to drive her to the Flats and let Jotham Powell take the lumber to Starkfield, and at first he could not think of a pretext for not doing so; then he said: 'I'd take you over myself, only I've got to collect the cash for the lumber.'

As soon as the words were spoken he regretted them, not only because they were untrue – there being no prospect of his receiving cash payment from Hale – but also because he knew from experience the imprudence of letting Zeena think he was in funds on the eve of one of her therapeutic excursions. At the moment, however, his one desire was to avoid the long drive with her behind the ancient sorrel who never went out of a walk.

Zeena made no reply: she did not seem to hear what he had said. She had already pushed her plate aside, and was measuring out a draught from a large bottle at her elbow.

'It ain't done me a speck of good, but I guess I might as well use it up,' she remarked; adding, as she pushed the empty bottle toward Mattie: 'If you can get the taste out it'll do for pickles.'

CHAPTER FOUR

As soon as his wife had driven off Ethan took his coat and cap from the peg. Mattie was washing up the dishes, humming one of the dance tunes of the night before. He said 'So long, Matt,' and she answered gaily, 'So long, Ethan;' and that was all.

It was warm and bright in the kitchen. The sun slanted through the south window on the girl's moving figure, on the cat dozing in a chair, and on the geraniums brought in from the doorway, where Ethan had planted them in the summer to 'make a garden' for Mattie. He would have liked to linger on, watching her tidy up and then settle down to her sewing; but he wanted still more to get the hauling done and be back at the farm before night.

All the way down to the village he continued to think of his return to Mattie. The kitchen was a poor place, not spruce and shining as his mother had kept it in his boyhood; but it was surprising what a homelike look the mere fact of Zeena's absence gave it. And he pictured what it would be like that evening, when he and Mattie were there after supper. For the first time they would be alone together indoors, and they would sit there, one on each side of the stove, like a married couple, he in his stocking feet and smoking his pipe, she laughing and talking in that funny way she had, which was always as new to him as if he had never heard her before.

The sweetness of the picture, and the relief of knowing that his fears of 'trouble' with Zeena were unfounded, sent up his spirits with a rush, and he, who was usually so silent, whistled and sang aloud as he drove through the snowy fields. There was in him a slumbering spark of sociability which the long Starkfield winters had not yet extinguished. By nature grave and inarticulate, he admired recklessness and gaiety in others and was warmed to the marrow by friendly human intercourse. At Worcester, though he had the name of keeping to himself and not being much of a hand at a good time, he had secretly gloried in being clapped on the back and hailed as 'Old Ethe' or 'Old Stiff'; and the cessation of such familiarities had increased the chill of his return to Starkfield.

There the silence had deepened about him year by year. Left alone, after his father's accident, to carry the burden of farm and mill, he had had no time for convivial loiterings in the village; and when his mother fell ill the loneliness of the house grew more oppressive than that of the fields. His mother had been a talker in her day, but after her 'trouble' the sound of her voice was seldom heard, though she had not lost the power of speech. Sometimes, in the long winter evenings, when in desperation her son asked her why she didn't 'say something', she would lift a finger and answer: 'Because I'm listening;' and on stormy nights, when the loud wind was about the house, she would complain, if he spoke to her: 'They're talking so out there that I can't hear you.'

It was only when she drew toward her last illness, and his cousin Zenobia Pierce came over from the next valley to help him nurse her, that human speech was heard again in the house. After the mortal silence of his long imprisonment Zeena's volubility was music in his ears. He felt that he might have 'gone like his mother' if the sound of a new voice had not come to steady him. Zeena seemed to understand his case at a glance. She laughed at him for not knowing the simplest sickbed duties and told him to 'go right along out' and leave her to see to things. The mere fact of obeying her orders, of feeling free to go about his business again and talk with other men, restored his shaken balance and magnified his sense of what he owed her. Her efficiency shamed and dazzled him. She seemed to possess by instinct all the household wisdom that his long apprenticeship had not instilled in him. When the end came it was she who had to tell him to hitch up and go for the undertaker, and she thought it 'funny' that he had not settled beforehand who was to have his mother's clothes and the sewing-machine. After the funeral, when he saw her preparing to go away, he was seized with an unreasoning dread of being left alone on the farm; and before he knew what he was doing he had asked her to stay there with him. He had often thought since that it would not have happened if his mother had died in spring instead of winter . . .

When they married it was agreed that, as soon as he could straighten out the difficulties resulting from Mrs Frome's long illness, they would sell the farm and sawmill and try their luck in a large town. Ethan's love of nature did not take the form of a taste for agriculture. He had always wanted to be an engineer, and to live in towns, where there were lectures and big libraries and 'fellows doing things'. A slight engineering job in Florida, put in his way during his period of study at Worcester, increased his faith in his ability as well as his eagerness to see the world; and he felt sure that, with a 'smart' wife like Zeena, it would not be long before he had made himself a place in it.

Zeena's native village was slightly larger and nearer to the railway than Starkfield, and she had let her husband see from the first that life on an isolated farm was not what she had expected when she married. But purchasers were slow in coming, and while he waited for them Ethan learned the impossibility of transplanting her. She chose to look down on Starkfield, but she could not have lived in a place which looked down on her. Even Bettsbridge or Shadd's Falls would not have been sufficiently aware of her, and in the greater cities which attracted Ethan she would have suffered a complete loss of identity. And within a year of their marriage she developed the 'sickliness' which had since made her notable even in a community rich in pathological instances. When she came to take care of his mother she had seemed to Ethan like the very genius of health, but he soon saw that her skill as a nurse had been acquired by the absorbed observation of her own symptoms.

Then she too fell silent. Perhaps it was the inevitable effect of life on the farm, or perhaps, as she sometimes said, it was because Ethan 'never listened'. The charge was not wholly unfounded. When she spoke it was only to complain, and to complain of things not in his power to remedy; and to check a tendency to impatient retort he had first formed the habit of not answering her, and finally of thinking of other things while she talked. Of late, however, since he had had reasons for observing her more closely, her silence had begun to trouble him. He recalled his mother's growing taciturnity, and wondered if Zeena were also turning 'queer'. Women did, he knew. Zeena, who had at her fingers' ends the pathological chart of the whole region, had cited many cases of the kind while she was nursing his mother; and he himself knew of certain lonely farm-houses in the neighbourhood where stricken creatures pined, and of others where sudden tragedy had come of their presence. At times, looking at Zeena's shut face, he felt the chill of such forebodings. At other times her silence seemed deliberately assumed to conceal far-reaching intentions, mysterious conclusions drawn from suspicions and resentments impossible to guess. That supposition was even more disturbing than the other; and it was the one which had come to him the night before, when he had seen her standing in the kitchen door.

Now her departure for Bettsbridge had once more eased his mind, and all his thoughts were on the prospect of his evening with Mattie. Only one thing weighed on him, and that was his having told Zeena that he was to receive cash for the lumber. He foresaw so clearly the consequences of this imprudence that with considerable reluctance he decided to ask Andrew Hale for a small advance on his load.

When Ethan drove into Hale's yard the builder was just getting out of his sleigh.

'Hello, Ethe!' he said. 'This comes handy.'

Andrew Hale was a ruddy man with a big grey moustache and a stubbly double chin unconstrained by a collar; but his scrupulously clean shirt was always fastened by a small diamond stud. This display of opulence was misleading, for though he did a fairly good business it was known that his easygoing habits and the demands of his large family frequently kept him what Starkfield called 'behind'. He was an old friend of Ethan's family, and his house one of the few to which Zeena occasionally went, drawn there by the fact that Mrs Hale, in her youth, had done more 'doctoring' than any other woman in Starkfield, and was still a recognised authority on symptoms and treatment.

Hale went up to the greys and patted their sweating flanks.

'Well, sir,' he said, 'you keep them two as if they was pets.'

Ethan set about unloading the logs and when he had finished his job he pushed open the glazed door of the shed which the builder used as his office. Hale sat with his feet up on the stove, his back propped against a battered desk strewn with papers: the place, like the man, was warm, genial and untidy.

'Sit right down and thaw out,' he greeted Ethan.

The latter did not know how to begin, but at length he managed to bring out his request for an advance of fifty dollars. The blood rushed to his thin skin under the sting of Hale's astonishment. It was the builder's custom to pay at the end of three months, and there was no precedent between the two men for a cash settlement.

Ethan felt that if he had pleaded an urgent need Hale might have made shift to pay him; but pride, and an instinctive prudence, kept him from resorting to this argument. After his father's death it had taken time to get his head above water, and he did not want Andrew Hale, or anyone else in Starkfield, to think he was going under again. Besides, he hated lying; if he wanted the money he wanted it, and it was nobody's business to ask why. He therefore made his demand with the awkwardness of a proud man who will not admit to himself that he is stooping; and he was not much surprised at Hale's refusal.

The builder refused genially, as he did everything else: he treated the matter as something in the nature of a practical joke, and wanted to know if Ethan meditated buying a grand piano or adding a 'cupolo'[25] to his house; offering, in the latter case, to give his services free of cost.

Ethan's arts were soon exhausted, and after an embarrassed pause he wished Hale good-day and opened the door of the office. As he passed out the builder suddenly called after him: 'See here – you ain't in a tight place, are you?'

'Not a bit,' Ethan's pride retorted before his reason had time to intervene.

'Well, that's good! Because I *am*, a shade. Fact is, I was going to ask you to give me a little extra time on that payment. Business is pretty slack, to begin with, and then I'm fixing up a little house for Ned and Ruth when they're married. I'm glad to do it for 'em, but it costs.' His look appealed to Ethan for sympathy. 'The young people like things nice. You know how it is yourself: it's not so long ago since you fixed up your own place for Zeena.'

Ethan left the greys in Hale's stable and went about some other business in the village. As he walked away the builder's last phrase lingered in his ears, and he reflected grimly that his seven years with Zeena seemed to Starkfield 'not so long'.

The afternoon was drawing to an end, and here and there a lighted pane spangled the cold grey dusk and made the snow look whiter. The bitter weather had driven everyone indoors and Ethan had the long rural street to himself. Suddenly he heard the brisk play of sleigh-bells and a cutter passed him, drawn by a free-going horse. Ethan recognised Michael Eady's roan colt, and young Denis Eady, in a handsome new fur cap, leaned forward and waved a greeting. 'Hello, Ethe!' he shouted and spun on.

The cutter was going in the direction of the Frome farm, and Ethan's heart contracted as he listened to the dwindling bells. What more likely than that Denis Eady had heard of Zeena's departure for Bettsbridge, and was profiting by the opportunity to spend an hour with Mattie? Ethan was ashamed of the storm of jealousy in his breast. It seemed unworthy of the girl that his thoughts of her should be so violent.

He walked on to the church corner and entered the shade of the Varnum spruces, where he had stood with her the night before. As he passed into their gloom he saw an indistinct outline just ahead of him. At his approach it melted for an instant into two separate shapes and then conjoined again, and he heard a kiss, and a half-laughing 'Oh!' provoked by the discovery of his presence. Again the outline hastily disunited and the Varnum gate slammed on one half while the other hurried on ahead of him. Ethan smiled at the discomfiture he had caused. What did it matter to Ned Hale and Ruth Varnum if they were caught kissing each other? Everybody in Starkfield knew they were engaged. It pleased Ethan to have surprised a pair of lovers on the spot where he and Mattie had stood with such a thirst for each other in their hearts; but he felt a pang at the thought that these two need not hide their happiness.

He fetched the greys from Hale's stable and started on his long climb back to the farm. The cold was less sharp than earlier in the day and a thick fleecy sky threatened snow for the morrow. Here and there a star pricked through, showing behind it a deep well of blue. In an hour or two the moon would push over the ridge behind the farm, burn a gold-edged rent in the clouds, and then be swallowed by them. A mournful peace hung on the fields, as though they felt the relaxing grasp of the cold and stretched themselves in their long winter sleep.

Ethan's ears were alert for the jingle of sleigh-bells, but not a sound broke the silence of the lonely road. As he drew near the farm he saw, through the thin screen of larches at the gate, a light twinkling in the house above him. 'She's up in her room,' he said to himself, 'fixing herself up for supper;' and he remembered Zeena's sarcastic stare when Mattie, on the evening of her arrival, had come down to supper with smoothed hair and a ribbon at her neck.

He passed by the graves on the knoll and turned his head to glance at one of the older headstones, which had interested him deeply as a boy because it bore his name.

SACRED TO THE MEMORY OF
ETHAN FROME AND ENDURANCE HIS WIFE,
WHO DWELLED TOGETHER IN PEACE
FOR FIFTY YEARS

He used to think that fifty years sounded like a long time to live together, but now it seemed to him that they might pass in a flash. Then, with a sudden dart of irony, he wondered if, when their turn came, the same epitaph would be written over him and Zeena.

He opened the barn door and craned his head into the obscurity, half-fearing to discover Denis Eady's roan colt in the stall beside the sorrel. But the old horse was there alone, mumbling his crib with toothless jaws, and Ethan whistled cheerfully while he bedded down the greys and shook an extra measure of oats into their mangers. His was not a tuneful throat, but harsh melodies burst from it as he locked the barn and sprang up the hill to the house. He reached the kitchen porch and turned the door handle; but the door did not yield to his touch.

Startled at finding it locked he rattled the handle violently; then he reflected that Mattie was alone and that it was natural she should barricade herself at nightfall. He stood in the darkness expecting to hear her step. It did not come, and after vainly straining his ears he called out in a voice that shook with joy: 'Hello, Matt!'

Silence answered; but in a minute or two he caught a sound on the stairs and saw a line of light about the door-frame, as he had seen it the night before. So strange was the precision with which the incidents of the previous evening were repeating themselves that he half expected, when he heard the key turn, to see his wife before him on the threshold; but the door opened, and Mattie faced him.

She stood just as Zeena had stood, a lifted lamp in her hand, against the black background of the kitchen. She held the light at the same level, and it drew out with the same distinctness her slim young throat and the brown wrist no bigger than a child's. Then, striking upward, it threw a lustrous fleck on her lips, edged her eyes with velvet shade, and laid a milky whiteness above the black curve of her brows.

She wore her usual dress of darkish stuff, and there was no bow at her neck; but through her hair she had run a streak of crimson ribbon. This tribute to the unusual transformed and glorified her. She seemed to Ethan taller, fuller, more womanly in shape and motion. She stood aside, smiling silently, while he entered, and then moved away from him with something soft and flowing in her gait. She set the lamp on the table, and he saw that it was carefully laid for supper, with fresh doughnuts, stewed blueberries and his favourite pickles in a dish of gay red glass. A bright fire glowed in the stove and the cat lay stretched before it, watching the table with a drowsy eye.

Ethan was suffocated with the sense of well-being. He went out into the passage to hang up his coat and pull off his wet boots. When he came back Mattie had set the teapot on the table and the cat was rubbing itself persuasively against her ankles.

'Why, puss! I nearly tripped over you,' she cried, the laughter sparkling through her lashes.

Again Ethan felt a sudden twinge of jealousy. Could it be his coming that gave her such a kindled face?

'Well, Matt, any visitors?' he threw off, stooping down carelessly to examine the fastening of the stove.

She nodded and laughed, 'Yes, one', and he felt a blackness settling on his brows.

'Who was that?' he questioned, raising himself up to slant a glance at her beneath his scowl.

Her eyes danced with malice. 'Why, Jotham Powell. He came in after he got back, and asked for a drop of coffee before he went down home.'

The blackness lifted and light flooded Ethan's brain. 'That all? Well, I hope you made out to let him have it.' And after a pause he felt it right to add: 'I suppose he got Zeena over to the Flats all right?'

'Oh, yes; in plenty of time.'

The name threw a chill between them, and they stood a moment looking sideways at each other before Mattie said with a shy laugh, 'I guess it's about time for supper.'

They drew their seats up to the table, and the cat, unbidden, jumped between them into Zeena's empty chair. 'Oh, puss!' said Mattie, and they laughed again.

Ethan, a moment earlier, had felt himself on the brink of eloquence; but the mention of Zeena had paralysed him. Mattie seemed to feel the contagion of his embarrassment, and sat with downcast lids, sipping her tea, while he feigned an insatiable appetite for doughnuts and sweet pickles. At last, after casting about for an effective opening, he took a long gulp of tea, cleared his throat, and said: 'Looks as if there'd be more snow.'

She feigned great interest. 'Is that so? Do you suppose it'll inter- fere with Zeena's getting back?' She flushed red as the question escaped her, and hastily set down the cup she was lifting.

Ethan reached over for another helping of pickles. 'You never can tell, this time of year, it drifts so bad on the Flats.' The name had benumbed him again, and once more he felt as if Zeena were in the room between them.

'Oh, puss, you're too greedy!' Mattie cried.

The cat, unnoticed, had crept up on muffled paws from Zeena's seat to the table, and was stealthily elongating its body in the direction of the milk-jug, which stood between Ethan and Mattie. The two leaned forward at the same moment and their hands met on the handle of the jug. Mattie's hand was underneath, and Ethan kept his clasped on it a moment longer than was necessary. The cat, profiting by this unusual demonstration, tried to effect an unnoticed retreat, and in doing so backed into the pickle-dish, which fell to the floor with a crash.

Mattie, in an instant, had sprung from her chair and was down on her knees by the fragments.

'Oh, Ethan, Ethan – it's all to pieces! What will Zeena say?'

But this time his courage was up. 'Well, she'll have to say it to the cat, anyway!' he rejoined with a laugh, kneeling down at Mattie's side to scrape up the swimming pickles.

She lifted stricken eyes to him. 'Yes, but, you see, she never meant it should be used, not even when there was company; and I had to get up on the stepladder to reach it down from the top shelf of the china-closet, where she keeps it with all her best things, and of course she'll want to know why I did it – '

The case was so serious that it called forth all of Ethan's latent resolution.

'She needn't know anything about it if you keep quiet. I'll get another just like it tomorrow. Where did it come from? I'll go to Shadd's Falls for it if I have to!'

'Oh, you'll never get another even there! It was a wedding present – don't you remember? It came all the way from Phila-delphia, from Zeena's aunt that married the minister. That's why she wouldn't ever use it. Oh, Ethan, Ethan, what in the world shall I do?'

She began to cry, and he felt as if every one of her tears were pouring over him like burning lead. 'Don't, Matt, don't – oh, *don't*!' he implored her.

She struggled to her feet, and he rose and followed her helplessly while she spread out the pieces of glass on the kitchen dresser. It seemed to him as if the shattered fragments of their evening lay there.

'Here, give them to me,' he said in a voice of sudden authority.

She drew aside, instinctively obeying his tone. 'Oh, Ethan, what are you going to do?'

Without replying he gathered the pieces of glass into his broad palm and walked out of the kitchen to the passage. There he lit a candle-end, opened the china-closet, and, reaching his long arm up to the highest shelf, laid the pieces together with such accuracy of touch that a close inspection convinced him of the impossibility of detecting from below that the dish was broken. If he glued it together the next morning months might elapse before his wife noticed what had happened, and meanwhile he might after all be able to match the dish at Shadd's Falls or Bettsbridge. Having satisfied himself that there was no risk of immediate discovery he went back to the kitchen with a lighter step, and found Mattie disconsolately removing the last scraps of pickle from the floor.

'It's all right, Matt. Come back and finish supper,' he commanded her.

Completely reassured, she shone on him through tear-hung lashes, and his soul swelled with pride as he saw how his tone subdued her. She did not even ask what he had done. Except when he was steering a big log down the mountain to his mill he had never known such a thrilling sense of mastery.

CHAPTER FIVE

THEY FINISHED SUPPER, and while Mattie cleared the table Ethan went to look at the cows and then took a last turn about the house. The earth lay dark under a muffled sky and the air was so still that now and then he heard a lump of snow come thumping down from a tree far off on the edge of the wood-lot.

When he returned to the kitchen Mattie had pushed up his chair to the stove and seated herself near the lamp with a bit of sewing. The scene was just as he had dreamed of it that morning. He sat down, drew his pipe from his pocket and stretched his feet to the glow. His hard day's work in the keen air made him feel at once lazy and light of mood, and he had a confused sense of being in another world, where all was warmth and harmony and time could bring no change. The only drawback to his complete well-being was the fact that he could not see Mattie from where he sat; but he was too indolent to move and after a moment he said: 'Come over here and sit by the stove.'

Zeena's empty rocking-chair stood facing him. Mattie rose obediently, and seated herself in it. As her young brown head detached itself against the patchwork cushion that habitually framed his wife's gaunt countenance, Ethan had a momentary shock. It was almost as if the other face, the face of the superseded woman, had obliterated that of the intruder. After a moment Mattie seemed to be affected by the same sense of constraint. She changed her position, leaning forward to bend her head above her work, so that he saw only the foreshortened tip of her nose and the streak of red in her hair; then she slipped to her feet, saying 'I can't see to sew,' and went back to her chair by the lamp.

Ethan made a pretext of getting up to replenish the stove, and when he returned to his seat he pushed it sideways that he might get a view of her profile and of the lamplight falling on her hands. The cat, who had been a puzzled observer of these unusual movements, jumped up into Zeena's chair, rolled itself into a ball, and lay watching them with narrowed eyes.

Deep quiet sank on the room. The clock ticked above the dresser, a piece of charred wood fell now and then in the stove, and the faint sharp scent of the geraniums mingled with the odour of Ethan's smoke, which began to throw a blue haze about the lamp and to hang its greyish cobwebs in the shadowy corners of the room.

All constraint had vanished between the two, and they began to talk easily and simply. They spoke of everyday things, of the prospect of snow, of the next church sociable, of the loves and quarrels of Starkfield. The commonplace nature of what they said produced in Ethan an illusion of long-established intimacy which no outburst of emotion could have given, and he set his imagination adrift on the fiction that they had always spent their evenings thus and would always go on doing so . . .

'This is the night we were to have gone coasting, Matt,' he said at length, with the rich sense, as he spoke, that they could go on any other night they chose, since they had all time before them.

She smiled back at him. 'I guess you forgot!'

'No, I didn't forget; but it's as dark as Egypt outdoors. We might go tomorrow if there's a moon.'

She laughed with pleasure, her head tilted back, the lamplight sparkling on her lips and teeth. 'That would be lovely, Ethan!'

He kept his eyes fixed on her, marvelling at the way her face changed with each turn of their talk, like a wheatfield under a summer breeze. It was intoxicating to find such magic in his clumsy words, and he longed to try new ways of using it.

'Would you be scared to go down the Corbury road with me on a night like this?' he asked.

Her cheeks burned redder. 'I ain't any more scared than you are!'

'Well, *I'd* be scared, then; I wouldn't do it. That's an ugly corner down by the big elm. If a fellow didn't keep his eyes open he'd go plumb into it.' He luxuriated in the sense of protection and authority which his words conveyed. To prolong and intensify the feeling he added: 'I guess we're well enough here.'

She let her lids sink slowly, in the way he loved. 'Yes, we're well enough here,' she sighed.

Her tone was so sweet that he took the pipe from his mouth and drew his chair up to the table. Leaning forward, he touched the farther end of the strip of brown stuff that she was hemming. 'Say, Matt,' he began with a smile, 'what do you think I saw under the Varnum spruces, coming along home just now? I saw a friend of yours getting kissed.'

The words had been on his tongue all the evening, but now that he had spoken them they struck him as inexpressibly vulgar and out of place.

Mattie blushed to the roots of her hair and pulled her needle rapidly twice or thrice through her work, insensibly drawing the end of it away from him. 'I suppose it was Ruth and Ned,' she said in a low voice, as though he had suddenly touched on something grave.

Ethan had imagined that his allusion might open the way to the accepted pleasantries, and these perhaps in turn to a harmless caress, if only a mere touch on her hand. But now he felt as if her blush had set a flaming guard about her. He supposed it was his natural awkwardness that made him feel so. He knew that most young men made nothing at all of giving a pretty girl a kiss, and he remembered that the night before, when he had put his arm about Mattie, she had not resisted. But that had been out-of-doors, under the open irresponsible night. Now, in the warm lamplit room, with all its ancient implications of conformity and order, she seemed infinitely farther away from him and more unapproachable.

To ease his constraint he said: 'I suppose they'll be setting a date before long.'

'Yes. I shouldn't wonder if they got married some time along in the summer.' She pronounced the word *married* as if her voice caressed it. It seemed a rustling covert leading to enchanted glades. A pang shot through Ethan, and he said, twisting away from her in his chair: 'It'll be your turn next, I wouldn't wonder.'

She laughed a little uncertainly. 'Why do you keep on saying that?'

He echoed her laugh. 'I guess I do it to get used to the idea.'

He drew up to the table again and she sewed on in silence, with dropped lashes, while he sat in fascinated contemplation of the way in which her hands went up and down above the strip of stuff, just as he had seen a pair of birds make short perpendicular flights over a nest they were building. At length, without turning her head or lifting her lids, she said in a low tone: 'It's not because you think Zeena's got anything against me, is it?'

His former dread started up full-armed at the suggestion. 'Why, what do you mean?' he stammered.

She raised distressed eyes to his, her work dropping on the table between them. 'I don't know. I thought last night she seemed to have.'

'I'd like to know what,' he growled.

'Nobody can tell with Zeena.' It was the first time they had ever spoken so openly of her attitude toward Mattie, and the repetition of the name seemed to carry it to the farther corners of the room and send it back to them in long repercussions of sound. Mattie waited, as if to give the echo time to drop, and then went on: 'She hasn't said anything to *you*?'

He shook his head. 'No, not a word.'

She tossed her hair back from her forehead with a laugh. 'I guess I'm just nervous, then. I'm not going to think about it any more.'

'Oh, no – don't let's think about it, Matt!'

The sudden heat of his tone made her colour mount again, not with a rush, but gradually, delicately, like the reflection of a thought stealing slowly across her heart. She sat silent, her hands clasped on her work, and it seemed to him that a warm current flowed toward him along the strip of stuff that still lay unrolled between them. Cautiously he slid his hand palm-downward along the table till his fingertips touched the end of the stuff. A faint vibration of her lashes seemed to show that she was aware of his gesture, and that it had sent a counter-current back to her; and she let her hands lie motionless on the other end of the strip.

As they sat thus he heard a sound behind him and turned his head. The cat had jumped from Zeena's chair to dart at a mouse in the wainscot, and as a result of the sudden movement the empty chair had set up a spectral rocking.

'She'll be rocking in it herself this time tomorrow,' Ethan thought. 'I've been in a dream, and this is the only evening we'll ever have together.' The return to reality was as painful as the return to consciousness after taking an anaesthetic. His body and brain ached with indescribable weariness, and he could think of nothing to say or to do that should arrest the mad flight of the moments.

His alteration of mood seemed to have communicated itself to Mattie. She looked up at him languidly, as though her lids were weighted with sleep and it cost her an effort to raise them. Her glance fell on his hand, which now completely covered the end of her work and grasped it as if it were a part of herself. He saw a scarcely perceptible tremor cross her face, and without knowing what he did he stooped his head and kissed the bit of stuff in his hold. As his lips rested on it he felt it glide slowly from beneath them, and saw that Mattie had risen and was silently rolling up her work. She fastened it with a pin, and then, finding her thimble and scissors, put them with the roll of stuff into the box covered with fancy paper which he had once brought to her from Bettsbridge.

He stood up also, looking vaguely about the room. The clock above the dresser struck eleven.

'Is the fire all right?' she asked in a low voice.

He opened the door of the stove and poked aimlessly at the embers. When he raised himself again he saw that she was dragging toward the stove the old soap-box lined with carpet in which the cat made its bed. Then she recrossed the floor and lifted two of the geranium pots in her arms, moving them away from the cold window. He followed her and brought the other geraniums, the hyacinth bulbs in a cracked custard bowl and the German ivy trained over an old croquet hoop.

When these nightly duties were performed there was nothing left to do but to bring in the tin candlestick from the passage, light the candle and blow out the lamp. Ethan put the candlestick in Mattie's hand and she went out of the kitchen ahead of him, the light that she carried before her making her dark hair look like a drift of mist on the moon.

'Good-night, Matt,' he said as she put her foot on the first step of the stairs.

She turned and looked at him a moment. 'Good-night, Ethan,' she answered, and went up.

When the door of her room had closed on her he remembered that he had not even touched her hand.

CHAPTER SIX

THE NEXT MORNING at breakfast Jotham Powell was between them, and Ethan tried to hide his joy under an air of exaggerated indifference, lounging back in his chair to throw scraps to the cat, growling at the weather, and not so much as offering to help Mattie when she rose to clear away the dishes.

He did not know why he was so irrationally happy, for nothing was changed in his life or hers. He had not even touched the tip of her fingers or looked her full in the eyes. But their evening together had given him a vision of what life at her side might be, and he was glad now that he had done nothing to trouble the sweetness of the picture. He had a fancy that she knew what had restrained him . . .

There was a last load of lumber to be hauled to the village, and Jotham Powell – who did not work regularly for Ethan in winter – had come round to help with the job. But a wet snow, melting to sleet, had fallen in the night and turned the roads to glass. There was more wet in the air and it seemed likely to both men that the weather would 'milden' toward afternoon and make the going safer. Ethan therefore proposed to his assistant that they should load the sledge at the wood-lot, as they had done on the previous morning, and put off the 'teaming' to Starkfield till later in the day. This plan had the advantage of enabling him to send Jotham to the Flats after dinner to meet Zenobia, while he himself took the lumber down to the village.

He told Jotham to go out and harness up the greys, and for a moment he and Mattie had the kitchen to themselves. She had plunged the breakfast dishes into a tin dish-pan and was bending above it with her slim arms bared to the elbow, the steam from the hot water beading her forehead and tightening her rough hair into little brown rings like the tendrils on the traveller's joy.[26]

Ethan stood looking at her, his heart in his throat. He wanted to say: 'We shall never be alone again like this.' Instead, he reached down his tobacco-pouch from a shelf of the dresser, put it into his pocket and said: 'I guess I can make out to be home for dinner.'

She answered, 'All right, Ethan,' and he heard her singing over the dishes as he went.

As soon as the sledge was loaded he meant to send Jotham back to the farm and hurry on foot into the village to buy the glue for the pickle-dish. With ordinary luck he should have had time to carry out this plan; but everything went wrong from the start. On the way over to the wood-lot one of the greys slipped on a glare of ice and cut his knee; and when they got him up again Jotham had to go back to the barn for a strip of rag to bind the cut. Then, when the loading finally began, a sleety rain was coming down once more, and the tree trunks were so slippery that it took twice as long as usual to lift them and get them in place on the sledge. It was what Jotham called a sour morning for work, and the horses, shivering and stamping under their wet blankets, seemed to like it as little as the men. It was long past the dinner-hour when the job was done, and Ethan had to give up going to the village because he wanted to lead the injured horse home and wash the cut himself.

He thought that by starting out again with the lumber as soon as he had finished his dinner he might get back to the farm with the glue before Jotham and the old sorrel had had time to fetch Zenobia from the Flats; but he knew the chance was a slight one. It turned on the state of the roads and on the possible lateness of the Bettsbridge train. He remembered afterward, with a grim flash of self-derision, what importance he had attached to the weighing of these probabilities . . .

As soon as dinner was over he set out again for the wood-lot, not daring to linger till Jotham Powell left. The hired man was still drying his wet feet at the stove, and Ethan could only give Mattie a quick look as he said beneath his breath: 'I'll be back early.'

He fancied that she nodded her comprehension; and with that scant solace he had to trudge off through the rain.

He had driven his load half-way to the village when Jotham Powell overtook him, urging the reluctant sorrel toward the Flats. 'I'll have to hurry up to do it,' Ethan mused, as the sleigh dropped down ahead of him over the dip of the schoolhouse hill. He worked like ten at the unloading, and when it was over hastened on to Michael Eady's for the glue. Eady and his assistant were both 'down street', and young Denis, who seldom deigned to take their place, was lounging by the stove with a knot of the golden youth of Starkfield. They hailed Ethan with ironic compliment and offers of conviviality; but no one knew where to find the glue. Ethan, consumed with the longing for a last moment alone with Mattie, hung about impatiently while Denis made an ineffectual search in the obscurer corners of the store.

'Looks as if we were all sold out. But if you'll wait around till the old man comes along maybe he can put his hand on it.'

'I'm obliged to you, but I'll try if I can get it down at Mrs Homan's,' Ethan answered, burning to be gone.

Denis's commercial instinct compelled him to aver on oath that what Eady's store could not produce would never be found at the widow Homan's; but Ethan, heedless of this boast, had already climbed to the sledge and was driving on to the rival establishment. Here, after considerable search, and sympathetic questions as to what he wanted it for, and whether ordinary flour paste wouldn't do as well if she couldn't find it, the widow Homan finally hunted down her solitary bottle of glue to its hiding-place in a medley of cough lozenges and corset laces.

'I hope Zeena ain't broken anything she sets store by,' she called after him as he turned the greys toward home.

The fitful bursts of sleet had changed into a steady rain and the horses had heavy work even without a load behind them. Once or twice, hearing sleigh-bells, Ethan turned his head, fancying that Zeena and Jotham might overtake him; but the old sorrel was not in sight, and he set his face against the rain and urged on his ponderous pair.

The barn was empty when the horses turned into it and, after giving them the most perfunctory ministrations they had ever received from him, he strode up to the house and pushed open the kitchen door.

Mattie was there alone, as he had pictured her. She was bending over a pan on the stove; but at the sound of his step she turned with a start and sprang to him.

'See, here, Matt, I've got some stuff to mend the dish with! Let me get at it quick,' he cried, waving the bottle in one hand while he put her lightly aside; but she did not seem to hear him.

'Oh, Ethan – Zeena's come,' she said in a whisper, clutching his sleeve.

They stood and stared at each other, pale as culprits.

'But the sorrel's not in the barn!' Ethan stammered.

'Jotham Powell brought some goods over from the Flats for his wife, and he drove right on home with them,' she explained.

He gazed blankly about the kitchen, which looked cold and squalid in the rainy winter twilight.

'How is she?' he asked, dropping his voice to Mattie's whisper.

She looked away from him uncertainly. 'I don't know. She went right up to her room.'

'She didn't say anything?'

'No.'

Ethan let out his doubts in a low whistle and thrust the bottle back into his pocket. 'Don't fret; I'll come down and mend it in the night,' he said. He pulled on his wet coat again and went back to the barn to feed the greys.

While he was there Jotham Powell drove up with the sleigh, and when the horses had been attended to Ethan said to him: 'You might as well come back up for a bite.' He was not sorry to assure himself of Jotham's neutralising presence at the supper table, for Zeena was always 'nervous'[27] after a journey. But the hired man, though seldom loath to accept a meal not included in his wages, opened his stiff jaws to answer slowly: 'I'm obliged to you, but I guess I'll go along back.'

Ethan looked at him in surprise. 'Better come up and dry off. Looks as if there'd be something hot for supper.'

Jotham's facial muscles were unmoved by this appeal and, his vocabulary being limited, he merely repeated: 'I guess I'll go along back.'

To Ethan there was something vaguely ominous in this stolid rejection of free food and warmth, and he wondered what had happened on the drive to nerve Jotham to such stoicism. Perhaps Zeena had failed to see the new doctor or had not liked his counsels: Ethan knew that in such cases the first person she met was likely to be held responsible for her grievance.

When he re-entered the kitchen the lamp lit up the same scene of shining comfort as on the previous evening. The table had been as carefully laid, a clear fire glowed in the stove, the cat dozed in its warmth, and Mattie came forward carrying a plate of doughnuts.

She and Ethan looked at each other in silence; then she said, as she had said the night before: 'I guess it's about time for supper.'

CHAPTER SEVEN

ETHAN WENT OUT into the passage to hang up his wet garments. He listened for Zeena's step and, not hearing it, called her name up the stairs. She did not answer, and after a moment's hesitation he went up and opened her door. The room was almost dark, but in the obscurity he saw her sitting by the window, bolt upright, and knew by the rigidity of the outline projected against the pane that she had not taken off her travelling dress.

'Well, Zeena,' he ventured from the threshold.

She did not move, and he continued: 'Supper's about ready. Ain't you coming?'

She replied: 'I don't feel as if I could touch a morsel.'

It was the consecrated formula, and he expected it to be followed, as usual, by her rising and going down to supper. But she remained seated, and he could think of nothing more felicitous than: 'I presume you're tired after the long ride.'

Turning her head at this, she answered solemnly: 'I'm a great deal sicker than you think.'

Her words fell on his ear with a strange shock of wonder. He had often heard her pronounce them before – what if at last they were true?

He advanced a step or two into the dim room. 'I hope that's not so, Zeena,' he said.

She continued to gaze at him through the twilight with a mien of wan authority, as of one consciously singled out for a great fate. 'I've got complications,' she said.

Ethan knew the word for one of exceptional import. Almost everybody in the neighbourhood had 'troubles', frankly localised and specified; but only the chosen had 'complications'. To have them was in itself a distinction, though it was also, in most cases, a death-warrant. People struggled on for years with 'troubles', but they almost always succumbed to 'complications'.

Ethan's heart was jerking to and fro between two extremities of feeling, but for the moment compassion prevailed. His wife looked so hard and lonely, sitting there in the darkness with such thoughts.

'Is that what the new doctor told you?' he asked, instinctively lowering his voice.

'Yes. He says any regular doctor would want me to have an operation.'

Ethan was aware that, in regard to the important question of surgical intervention, the female opinion of the neighbourhood was divided, some glorying in the prestige conferred by operations while others shunned them as indelicate. Ethan, from motives of economy, had always been glad that Zeena was of the latter faction.

In the agitation caused by the gravity of her announcement he sought a consolatory short cut. 'What do you know about this doctor anyway? Nobody ever told you that before.'

He saw his blunder before she could take it up: she wanted sympathy, not consolation.

'I didn't need to have anybody tell me I was losing ground every day. Everybody but you could see it. And everybody in Bettsbridge knows about Dr Buck. He has his office in Worcester, and comes over once a fortnight to Shadd's Falls and Bettsbridge for consultations. Eliza Spears was wasting away with kidney trouble before she went to him, and now she's up and around, and singing in the choir.'

'Well, I'm glad of that. You must do just what he tells you,' Ethan answered sympathetically.

She was still looking at him. 'I mean to,' she said. He was struck by a new note in her voice. It was neither whining nor reproachful, but drily resolute.

'What does he want you should do?' he asked, with a mounting vision of fresh expenses.

'He wants I should have a hired girl. He says I oughtn't to have to do a single thing around the house.'

'A hired girl?' Ethan stood transfixed.

'Yes. And Aunt Martha found me one right off. Everybody said I was lucky to get a girl to come away out here, and I agreed to give her a dollar extry to make sure. She'll be over tomorrow afternoon.'

Wrath and dismay contended in Ethan. He had foreseen an immediate demand for money, but not a permanent drain on his scant resources. He no longer believed what Zeena had told him of the supposed seriousness of her state: he saw in her expedition to Bettsbridge only a plot hatched between herself and her Pierce relations to foist on him the cost of a servant; and for the moment wrath predominated.

'If you meant to engage a girl you ought to have told me before you started,' he said.

'How could I tell you before I started? How did I know what Dr Buck would say?'

'Oh, Dr Buck – ' Ethan's incredulity escaped in a short laugh. 'Did Dr Buck tell you how I was to pay her wages?'

Her voice rose furiously with his. 'No, he didn't. For I'd 'a' been ashamed to tell *him* that you grudged me the money to get back my health, when I lost it nursing your own mother!'

'*You* lost your health nursing mother?'

'Yes; and my folks all told me at the time you couldn't do no less than marry me after – '

'Zeena!'

Through the obscurity which hid their faces their thoughts seemed to dart at each other like serpents shooting venom. Ethan was seized with horror of the scene and shame at his own share in it. It was as senseless and savage as a physical fight between two enemies in the darkness.

He turned to the shelf above the chimney, groped for matches and lit the one candle in the room. At first its weak flame made no impression on the shadows; then Zeena's face stood grimly out against the uncurtained pane, which had turned from grey to black.

It was the first scene of open anger between the couple in their sad seven years together, and Ethan felt as if he had lost an irretrievable advantage in descending to the level of recrimination. But the practical problem was there and had to be dealt with.

'You know I haven't got the money to pay for a girl, Zeena. You'll have to send her back: I can't do it.'

'The doctor says it'll be my death if I go on slaving the way I've had to. He doesn't understand how I've stood it as long as I have.'

'Slaving! – ' He checked himself again. 'You shan't lift a hand, if he says so. I'll do everything round the house myself – '

She broke in: 'You're neglecting the farm enough already,' and this being true, he found no answer, and left her time to add ironically: 'Better send me over to the almshouse and have done with it . . . I guess there's been Fromes there afore now.'

The taunt burned into him, but he let it pass. 'I haven't got the money. That settles it.'

There was a moment's pause in the struggle, as though the combatants were testing their weapons. Then Zeena said in a level voice: 'I thought you were to get fifty dollars from Andrew Hale for that lumber.'

'Andrew Hale never pays under three months.' He had hardly spoken when he remembered the excuse he had made for not accompanying his wife to the station the day before; and the blood rose to his frowning brows.

'Why, you told me yesterday you'd fixed it up with him to pay cash down. You said that was why you couldn't drive me over to the Flats.'

Ethan had no suppleness in deceiving. He had never before been convicted of a lie, and all the resources of evasion failed him. 'I guess that was a misunderstanding,' he stammered.

'You ain't got the money?'

'No.'

'And you ain't going to get it?'

'No.'

'Well, I couldn't know that when I engaged the girl, could I?'

'No.' He paused to control his voice. 'But you know it now. I'm sorry, but it can't be helped. You're a poor man's wife, Zeena; but I'll do the best I can for you.'

For a while she sat motionless, as if reflecting, her arms stretched along the arms of her chair, her eyes fixed on vacancy. 'Oh, I guess we'll make out,' she said mildly.

The change in her tone reassured him. 'Of course we will! There's a whole lot more I can do for you, and Mattie – '

Zeena, while he spoke, seemed to be following out some elaborate mental calculation. She emerged from it to say: 'There'll be Mattie's board less, anyhow – '

Ethan, supposing the discussion to be over, had turned to go down to supper. He stopped short, not grasping what he heard. 'Mattie's board less – ?' he began.

Zeena laughed. It was an odd unfamiliar sound – he did not remember ever having heard her laugh before. 'You didn't suppose I was going to keep two girls, did you? No wonder you were scared at the expense!'

He still had but a confused sense of what she was saying. From the beginning of the discussion he had instinctively avoided the mention of Mattie's name, fearing he hardly knew what: criticism, complaints, or vague allusions to the imminent probability of her marrying. But the thought of a definite rupture had never come to him, and even now could not lodge itself in his mind.

'I don't know what you mean,' he said. 'Mattie Silver's not a hired girl. She's your relation.'

'She's a pauper that's hung on to us all after her father'd done his best to ruin us. I've kep' her here a whole year: it's somebody else's turn now.'

As the shrill words shot out Ethan heard a tap on the door, which he had drawn shut when he turned back from the threshold.

'Ethan – Zeena!' Mattie's voice sounded gaily from the landing, 'do you know what time it is? Supper's been ready half an hour.'

Inside the room there was a moment's silence; then Zeena called out from her seat: 'I'm not coming down to supper.'

'Oh, I'm sorry! Aren't you well? Shan't I bring you up a bite of something?'

Ethan roused himself with an effort and opened the door. 'Go along down, Matt. Zeena's just a little tired. I'm coming.'

He heard her 'All right!' and her quick step on the stairs; then he shut the door and turned back into the room. His wife's attitude was unchanged, her face inexorable, and he was seized with the despairing sense of his helplessness.

'You ain't going to do it, Zeena?'

'Do what?' she emitted between flattened lips.

'Send Mattie away – like this?'

'I never bargained to take her for life!'

He continued with rising vehemence: 'You can't put her out of the house like a thief – a poor girl without friends or money. She's done her best for you and she's got no place to go to. You may forget she's your kin but everybody else'll remember it. If you do a thing like that what do you suppose folks'll say of you?'

Zeena waited a moment, as if giving him time to feel the full force of the contrast between his own excitement and her composure. Then she replied in the same smooth voice: 'I know well enough what they say of my having kep' her here as long as I have.'

Ethan's hand dropped from the doorknob, which he had held clenched since he had drawn the door shut on Mattie. His wife's retort was like a knife-cut across the sinews and he felt suddenly weak and powerless. He had meant to humble himself, to argue that Mattie's keep didn't cost much, after all, that he could make out to buy a stove and fix up a place in the attic for the hired girl – but Zeena's words revealed the peril of such pleadings.

'You mean to tell her she's got to go – at once?' he faltered out, in terror of letting his wife complete her sentence.

As if trying to make him see reason she replied impartially: 'The girl will be over from Bettsbridge tomorrow, and I presume she's got to have somewheres to sleep.'

Ethan looked at her with loathing. She was no longer the listless creature who had lived at his side in a state of sullen self-absorption, but a mysterious alien presence, an evil energy secreted from the long years of silent brooding. It was the sense of his helplessness that sharpened his antipathy. There had never been anything in her that one could appeal to; but as long as he could ignore and command he had remained indifferent. Now she had mastered him and he abhorred her. Mattie was her relation, not his: there were no means by which he could compel her to keep the girl under her roof. All the long misery of his baffled past, of his youth of failure, hardship and vain effort, rose up in his soul in bitterness and seemed to take shape before him in the woman who at every turn had barred his way. She had taken everything else from him; and now she meant to take the one thing that made up for all the others. For a moment such a flame of hate rose in him that it ran down his arm and clenched his fist against her. He took a wild step forward and then stopped.

'You're – you're not coming down?' he said in a bewildered voice.

'No. I guess I'll lay down on the bed a little while,' she answered mildly; and he turned and walked out of the room.

In the kitchen Mattie was sitting by the stove, the cat curled up on her knees. She sprang to her feet as Ethan entered and carried the covered dish of meat pie to the table.

'I hope Zeena isn't sick?' she asked.

'No.'

She shone at him across the table. 'Well, sit right down then. You must be starving.' She uncovered the pie and pushed it over to him. So they were to have one more evening together, her happy eyes seemed to say!

He helped himself mechanically and began to eat; then disgust took him by the throat and he laid down his fork.

Mattie's tender gaze was on him and she marked the gesture.

'Why, Ethan, what's the matter? Don't it taste right?'

'Yes – it's first-rate. Only I – ' He pushed his plate away, rose from his chair, and walked around the table to her side. She started up with frightened eyes.

'Ethan, there's something wrong! I *knew* there was!'

She seemed to melt against him in her terror, and he caught her in his arms, held her fast there, felt her lashes beat his cheek like netted butterflies.

'What is it – what is it?' she stammered; but he had found her lips at last and was drinking unconsciousness of everything but the joy they gave him.

She lingered a moment, caught in the same strong current; then she slipped from him and drew back a step or two, pale and troubled. Her look smote him with compunction, and he cried out, as if he saw her drowning in a dream: 'You can't go, Matt! I'll never let you!'

'Go – go?' she stammered. 'Must I go?'

The words went on sounding between them as though a torch of warning flew from hand to hand through a black landscape.

Ethan was overcome with shame at his lack of self-control in flinging the news at her so brutally. His head reeled and he had to support himself against the table. All the while he felt as if he were still kissing her, and yet dying of thirst for her lips.

'Ethan, what has happened? Is Zeena mad with me?'

Her cry steadied him, though it deepened his wrath and pity. 'No, no,' he assured her, 'it's not that. But this new doctor has scared her about herself. You know she believes all they say the first time she sees them. And this one's told her she won't get well unless she lays up and don't do a thing about the house – not for months – '

He paused, his eyes wandering from her miserably. She stood silent a moment, drooping before him like a broken branch. She was so small and weak-looking that it wrung his heart; but suddenly she lifted her head and looked straight at him. 'And she wants somebody handier in my place? Is that it?'

'That's what she says tonight.'

'If she says it tonight she'll say it tomorrow.'

Both bowed to the inexorable truth: they knew that Zeena never changed her mind, and that in her case a resolve once taken was equivalent to an act performed.

There was a long silence between them; then Mattie said in a low voice: 'Don't be too sorry, Ethan.'

'Oh, God – oh, God,' he groaned. The glow of passion he had felt for her had melted to an aching tenderness. He saw her quick lids beating back the tears, and longed to take her in his arms and soothe her.

'You're letting your supper get cold,' she admonished him with a pale gleam of gaiety.

'Oh, Matt – Matt – where'll you go to?'

Her lids sank and a tremor crossed her face. He saw that for the first time the thought of the future came to her distinctly. 'I might get something to do over at Stamford,' she faltered, as if knowing that he knew she had no hope.

He dropped back into his seat and hid his face in his hands. Despair seized him at the thought of her setting out alone to renew the weary quest for work. In the only place where she was known she was surrounded by indifference or animosity; and what chance had she, inexperienced and untrained, among the million bread-seekers of the cities? There came back to him miserable tales he had heard at Worcester, and the faces of girls whose lives had begun as hopefully as Mattie's . . . It was not possible to think of such things without a revolt of his whole being. He sprang up suddenly.

'You can't go, Matt! I won't let you! She's always had her way, but I mean to have mine now – '

Mattie lifted her hand with a quick gesture, and he heard his wife's step behind him.

Zeena came into the room with her dragging down-at-the-heel step, and quietly took her accustomed seat between them.

'I felt a little mite better, and Dr Buck says I ought to eat all I can to keep my strength up, even if I ain't got any appetite,' she said in her flat whine, reaching across Mattie for the teapot. Her 'good' dress had been replaced by the black calico and brown knitted shawl which formed her daily wear, and with them she had put on her usual face and manner. She poured out her tea, added a great deal of milk to it, helped herself largely to pie and pickles, and made the familiar gesture of adjusting her false teeth before she began to eat. The cat rubbed itself ingratiatingly against her, and she said 'Good pussy,' stooped to stroke it and gave it a scrap of meat from her plate.

Ethan sat speechless, not pretending to eat, but Mattie nibbled valiantly at her food and asked Zeena one or two questions about her visit to Bettsbridge. Zeena answered in her everyday tone and, warming to the theme, regaled them with several vivid descriptions of intestinal disturbances among her friends and relatives. She looked straight at Mattie as she spoke, a faint smile deepening the vertical lines between her nose and chin.

When supper was over she rose from her seat and pressed her hand to the flat surface over the region of her heart. 'That pie of yours always sets a mite heavy, Matt,' she said, not ill-naturedly. She seldom abbreviated the girl's name, and when she did so it was always a sign of affability. 'I've a good mind to go and hunt up those stomach powders I got last year over in Springfield,' she continued. 'I ain't tried them for quite a while, and maybe they'll help the heartburn.'

Mattie lifted her eyes. 'Can't I get them for you, Zeena?' she ventured.

'No. They're in a place you don't know about,' Zeena answered darkly, with one of her secret looks.

She went out of the kitchen and Mattie, rising, began to clear the dishes from the table. As she passed Ethan's chair their eyes met and clung together desolately. The warm still kitchen looked as peaceful as the night before. The cat had sprung to Zeena's rocking-chair, and the heat of the fire was beginning to draw out the faint sharp scent of the geraniums. Ethan dragged himself wearily to his feet.

'I'll go out and take a look around,' he said, going toward the passage to get his lantern.

As he reached the door he met Zeena coming back into the room, her lips twitching with anger, a flush of excitement on her sallow face. The shawl had slipped from her shoulders and was dragging at her down-trodden heels, and in her hands she carried the fragments of the red glass pickle-dish.

'I'd like to know who done this,' she said, looking sternly from Ethan to Mattie. There was no answer, and she continued in a trembling voice: 'I went to get those powders I'd put away in father's old spectacle-case, top of the china-closet, where I keep the things I set store by, so's folks shan't meddle with them – ' Her voice broke, and two small tears hung on her lashless lids and ran slowly down her cheeks. 'It takes the stepladder to get at the top shelf, and I put Aunt Philura Maple's pickle-dish up there o' purpose when we was married, and it's never been down since, 'cept for the spring cleaning, and then I always lifted it with my own hands, so's 't shouldn't get broke.' She laid the fragments reverently on the table. 'I want to know who done this,' she quavered.

At the challenge Ethan turned back into the room and faced her. 'I can tell you, then. The cat done it.'

'The *cat*?'

'That's what I said.'

She looked at him hard, and then turned her eyes to Mattie, who was carrying the dish-pan to the table.

'I'd like to know how the cat got into my china-closet,' she said.

'Chasin' mice, I guess,' Ethan rejoined. 'There was a mouse round the kitchen all last evening.'

Zeena continued to look from one to the other; then she emitted her small strange laugh. 'I knew the cat was a smart cat,' she said in a high voice, 'but I didn't know he was smart enough to pick up the pieces of my pickle-dish and lay 'em edge to edge on the very shelf he knocked 'em off of.'

Mattie suddenly drew her arms out of the steaming water. 'It wasn't Ethan's fault, Zeena! The cat *did* break the dish; but I got it down from the china-closet, and I'm the one to blame for its getting broken.'

Zeena stood beside the ruin of her treasure, stiffening into a stony image of resentment, '*You* got down my pickle-dish – what for?'

A bright flush flew to Mattie's cheeks. 'I wanted to make the supper-table pretty,' she said.

'You wanted to make the supper-table pretty; and you waited till my back was turned, and took the thing I set most store by of anything I've got, and wouldn't never use it, not even when the minister come to dinner, or Aunt Martha Pierce come over from Bettsbridge – ' Zeena paused with a gasp, as if terrified by her own evocation of the sacrilege. 'You're a bad girl, Mattie Silver, and I always known it. It's the way your father begun, and I was warned of it when I took you, and I tried to keep my things where you couldn't get at 'em – and now you've took from me the one I cared for most of all – ' She broke off in a short spasm of sobs that passed and left her more than ever like a shape of stone.

'If I'd 'a' listened to folks, you'd 'a' gone before now, and this wouldn't 'a' happened,' she said; and gathering up the bits of broken glass she went out of the room as if she carried a dead body . . .

CHAPTER EIGHT

WHEN ETHAN WAS called back to the farm by his father's illness his mother gave him, for his own use, a small room behind the untenanted 'best parlour'. Here he had nailed up shelves for his books, built himself a box-sofa out of boards and a mattress, laid out his papers on a kitchen table, hung on the rough plaster wall an engraving of Abraham Lincoln[28] and a calendar with 'Thoughts from the Poets' and tried, with these meagre properties, to produce some likeness to the study of a minister who had been kind to him and lent him books when he was at Worcester. He still took refuge there in summer, but when Mattie came to live at the farm he had had to give her his stove, and consequently the room was uninhabitable for several months of the year.

To this retreat he descended as soon as the house was quiet and Zeena's steady breathing from the bed had assured him that there was to be no sequel to the scene in the kitchen. After Zeena's departure he and Mattie had stood speechless, neither seeking to approach the other. Then the girl had returned to her task of clearing up the kitchen for the night and he had taken his lantern and gone on his usual round outside the house. The kitchen was empty when he came back to it; but his tobacco-pouch and pipe had been laid on the table, and under them was a scrap of paper torn from the back of a seedsman's catalogue, on which three words were written: 'Don't trouble, Ethan.'

Going into his cold dark study he placed the lantern on the table and, stooping to its light, read the message again and again. It was the first time that Mattie had ever written to him, and the possession of the paper gave him a strange new sense of her nearness; yet it deepened his anguish by reminding him that henceforth they would have no other way of communicating with each other. For the life of her smile, the warmth of her voice, only cold paper and dead words!

Confused emotions of rebellion stormed in him. He was too young, too strong, too full of the sap of living, to submit so easily to the destruction of his hopes. Must he wear out all his years at the side of a bitter querulous woman? Other possibilities had been in him, possibilities sacrificed, one by one, to Zeena's narrow-mindedness and ignorance. And what good had come of it? She was a hundred times bitterer and more discontented than when he had married her: the one pleasure left her was to inflict pain on him. All the healthy instincts of self-defence rose up in him against such waste . . .

He bundled himself into his old coon-skin coat and lay down on the box-sofa to think. Under his cheek he felt a hard object with strange protuberances. It was a cushion which Zeena had made for him when they were engaged – the only piece of needlework he had ever seen her do. He flung it across the floor and propped his head against the wall . . .

He knew a case of a man over the mountain – a young fellow of about his own age – who had escaped from just such a life of misery by going West with the girl he cared for. His wife had divorced him, and he had married the girl and prospered. Ethan had seen the couple the summer before at Shadd's Falls, where they had come to visit relatives. They had a little girl with fair curls, who wore a gold locket and was dressed like a princess. The deserted wife had not done badly either. Her husband had given her the farm and she had managed to sell it, and with that and the alimony she had started a lunch-room at Bettsbridge and bloomed into activity and importance. Ethan was fired by the thought. Why should he not leave with Mattie the next day, instead of letting her go alone? He would hide his valise under the seat of the sleigh, and Zeena would suspect nothing till she went upstairs for her afternoon nap and found a letter on the bed . . .

His impulses were still near the surface, and he sprang up, re-lit the lantern, and sat down at the table. He rummaged in the drawer for a sheet of paper, found one and began to write.

'Zeena, I've done all I could for you, and I don't see as it's been any use. I don't blame you, nor I don't blame myself. Maybe both of us will do better separate. I'm going to try my luck West, and you can sell the farm and mill, and keep the money – '

His pen paused on the word, which brought home to him the relentless conditions of his lot. If he gave the farm and mill to Zeena what would be left him to start his own life with? Once in the West he was sure of picking up work – he would not have feared to try his chance alone. But with Mattie depending on him the case was different. And what of Zeena's fate? Farm and mill were mortgaged to the limit of their value, and even if she found a purchaser – in itself an unlikely chance – it was doubtful if she could clear a thousand dollars on the sale. Meanwhile, how could she keep the farm going? It was only by incessant labour and personal supervision that Ethan drew a meagre living from his land, and his wife, even if she were in better health than she imagined, could never carry such a burden alone.

Well, she could go back to her people, then, and see what they would do for her. It was the fate she was forcing on Mattie – why not let her try it herself? By the time she had discovered his whereabouts, and brought a suit for divorce, he would probably – wherever he was – be earning enough to pay her sufficient alimony. And the alternative was to let Mattie go forth alone, with far less hope of ultimate provision . . .

He had scattered the contents of the table-drawer in his search for a sheet of paper, and as he took up his pen his eye fell on an old copy of the *Bettsbridge Eagle*. The advertising sheet was folded uppermost, and he read the seductive words: 'Trips to the West: Reduced Rates'.

He drew the lantern nearer and eagerly scanned the fares; then the paper fell from his hand and he pushed aside his unfinished letter. A moment ago he had wondered what he and Mattie were to live on when they reached the West; now he saw that he had not even the money to take her there. Borrowing was out of the question: six months before he had given his only security to raise funds for necessary repairs to the mill, and he knew that without security no one at Starkfield would lend him ten dollars. The inexorable facts closed in on him like prison-warders handcuffing a convict. There was no way out – none. He was a prisoner for life, and now his one ray of light was to be extinguished.

He crept back heavily to the sofa, stretching himself out with limbs so leaden that he felt as if they would never move again. Tears rose in his throat and slowly burned their way to his lids.

As he lay there, the window-pane that faced him, growing gradually lighter, inlaid upon the darkness a square of moon-suffused sky. A crooked tree-branch crossed it, a branch of the apple tree under which, on summer evenings, he had sometimes found Mattie sitting when he came up from the mill. Slowly the rim of the rainy vapours caught fire and burnt away, and a pure moon swung into the blue. Ethan, rising on his elbow, watched the landscape whiten and shape itself under the sculpture of the moon. This was the night on which he was to have taken Mattie coasting, and there hung the lamp to light them! He looked out at the slopes bathed in lustre, the silver-edged darkness of the woods, the spectral purple of the hills against the sky, and it seemed as though all the beauty of the night had been poured out to mock his wretchedness . . .

He fell asleep, and when he woke the chill of the winter dawn was in the room. He felt cold and stiff and hungry, and ashamed of being hungry. He rubbed his eyes and went to the window. A red sun stood over the grey rim of the fields, behind trees that looked black and brittle. He said to himself: 'This is Matt's last day,' and tried to think what the place would be without her.

As he stood there he heard a step behind him and she entered.

'Oh, Ethan – were you here all night?'

She looked so small and pinched, in her poor dress, with the red scarf wound about her, and the cold light turning her paleness sallow, that Ethan stood before her without speaking.

'You must be frozen,' she went on, fixing lustreless eyes on him.

He drew a step nearer. 'How did you know I was here?'

'Because I heard you go downstairs again after I went to bed, and I listened all night, and you didn't come up.'

All his tenderness rushed to his lips. He looked at her and said: 'I'll come right along and make up the kitchen fire.'

They went back to the kitchen, and he fetched the coal and kindlings and cleared out the stove for her, while she brought in the milk and the cold remains of the meat pie. When warmth began to radiate from the stove, and the first ray of sunlight lay on the kitchen floor, Ethan's dark thoughts melted in the mellower air. The sight of Mattie going about her work as he had seen her on so many mornings made it seem impossible that she should ever cease to be a part of the scene. He said to himself that he had doubtless exaggerated the significance of Zeena's threats, and that she too, with the return of daylight, would come to a saner mood.

He went up to Mattie as she bent above the stove, and laid his hand on her arm. 'I don't want you should trouble either,' he said, looking down into her eyes with a smile.

She flushed up warmly and whispered back: 'No, Ethan, I ain't going to trouble.'

'I guess things'll straighten out,' he added. There was no answer but a quick throb of her lids, and he went on: 'She ain't said anything this morning?'

'No. I haven't seen her yet.'

'Don't you take any notice when you do.'

With this injunction he left her and went out to the cow-barn. He saw Jotham Powell walking up the hill through the morning mist, and the familiar sight added to his growing conviction of security.

As the two men were clearing out the stalls Jotham rested on his pitchfork to say: 'Dan'l Byrne's goin' over to the Flats today noon, an' he c'd take Mattie's trunk along, and make it easier ridin' when I take her over in the sleigh.'

Ethan looked at him blankly, and he continued: 'Mis' Frome said the new girl'd be at the Flats at five, and I was to take Mattie then, so's 't she could ketch the six o'clock train for Stamford.'

Ethan felt the blood drumming in his temples. He had to wait a moment before he could find voice to say: 'Oh, it ain't so sure about Mattie's going – '

'That so?' said Jotham indifferently; and they went on with their work.

When they returned to the kitchen the two women were already at breakfast. Zeena had an air of unusual alertness and activity. She drank two cups of coffee and fed the cat with the scraps left in the pie-dish; then she rose from her seat and, walking over to the window, snipped two or three yellow leaves from the geraniums. 'Aunt Martha's ain't got a faded leaf on 'em; but they pine away when they ain't cared for,' she said reflectively. Then she turned to Jotham and asked: 'What time'd you say Dan'l Byrne'd be along?'

The hired man threw a hesitating glance at Ethan. 'Round about noon,' he said.

Zeena turned to Mattie. 'That trunk of yours is too heavy for the sleigh, and Dan'l Byrne'll be round to take it over to the Flats,' she said.

'I'm much obliged to you, Zeena,' said Mattie.

'I'd like to go over things with you first,' Zeena continued in an unperturbed voice. 'I know there's a huckabuck towel[29] missing; and I can't make out what you done with that match-safe 't used to stand behind the stuffed owl in the parlour.'

She went out, followed by Mattie, and when the men were alone Jotham said to his employer: 'I guess I better let Dan'l come round, then.'

Ethan finished his usual morning tasks about the house and barn; then he said to Jotham: 'I'm going down to Starkfield. Tell them not to wait dinner.'

The passion of rebellion had broken out in him again. That which had seemed incredible in the sober light of day had really come to pass, and he was to assist as a helpless spectator at Mattie's banishment. His manhood was humbled by the part he was compelled to play and by the thought of what Mattie must think of him. Confused impulses struggled in him as he strode along to the village. He had made up his mind to do something, but he did not know what it would be.

The early mist had vanished and the fields lay like a silver shield under the sun. It was one of the days when the glitter of winter shines through a pale haze of spring. Every yard of the road was alive with Mattie's presence, and there was hardly a branch against the sky or a tangle of brambles on the bank in which some bright shred of memory was not caught. Once, in the stillness, the call of a bird in a mountain ash was so like her laughter that his heart tightened and then grew large; and all these things made him see that something must be done at once.

Suddenly it occurred to him that Andrew Hale, who was a kind-hearted man, might be induced to reconsider his refusal and advance a small sum on the lumber if he were told that Zeena's ill-health made it necessary to hire a servant. Hale, after all, knew enough of Ethan's situation to make it possible for the latter to renew his appeal without too much loss of pride; and, moreover, how much did pride count in the ebullition of passions in his breast?

The more he considered his plan the more hopeful it seemed. If he could get Mrs Hale's ear he felt certain of success, and with fifty dollars in his pocket nothing could keep him from Mattie . . .

His first object was to reach Starkfield before Hale had started for his work; he knew the carpenter had a job down the Corbury road and was likely to leave his house early. Ethan's long strides grew more rapid with the accelerated beat of his thoughts, and as he reached the foot of School House Hill he caught sight of Hale's sleigh in the distance. He hurried forward to meet it, but as it drew nearer he saw that it was driven by the carpenter's youngest boy and that the figure at his side, looking like a large upright cocoon in spectacles, was that of Mrs Hale. Ethan signed to them to stop, and Mrs Hale leaned forward, her pink wrinkles twinkling with benevolence.

'Mr Hale? Why, yes, you'll find him down home now. He ain't going to his work this forenoon. He woke up with a touch o' lumbago, and I just made him put on one of old Dr Kidder's plasters and set right up into the fire.'

Beaming maternally on Ethan, she bent over to add: 'I on'y just heard from Mr Hale 'bout Zeena's going over to Bettsbridge to see that new doctor. I'm real sorry she's feeling so bad again! I hope he thinks he can do something for her. I don't know anybody round here's had more sickness than Zeena. I always tell Mr Hale I don't know what she'd 'a' done if she hadn't 'a' had you to look after her; and I used to say the same thing 'bout your mother. You've had an awful mean time, Ethan Frome.'

She gave him a last nod of sympathy while her son chirped to the horse; and Ethan, as she drove off, stood in the middle of the road and stared after the retreating sleigh.

It was a long time since anyone had spoken to him as kindly as Mrs Hale. Most people were either indifferent to his troubles, or disposed to think it natural that a young fellow of his age should have carried without repining the burden of three crippled lives. But Mrs Hale had said, 'You've had an awful mean time, Ethan Frome,' and he felt less alone with his misery. If the Hales were sorry for him they would surely respond to his appeal . . .

He started down the road toward their house, but at the end of a few yards he pulled up sharply, the blood in his face. For the first time, in the light of the words he had just heard, he saw what he was about to do. He was planning to take advantage of the Hales' sympathy to obtain money from them on false pretences. That was a plain statement of the cloudy purpose which had driven him in headlong to Starkfield.

With the sudden perception of the point to which his madness had carried him, the madness fell and he saw his life before him as it was. He was a poor man, the husband of a sickly woman, whom his desertion would leave alone and destitute; and even if he had had the heart to desert her he could have done so only by deceiving two kindly people who had pitied him.

He turned and walked slowly back to the farm.

CHAPTER NINE

At the kitchen door Daniel Byrne sat in his sleigh behind a big-boned grey who pawed the snow and swung his long head restlessly from side to side.

Ethan went into the kitchen and found his wife by the stove. Her head was wrapped in her shawl, and she was reading a book called *Kidney Troubles and Their Cure* on which he had had to pay extra postage only a few days before.

Zeena did not move or look up when he entered and after a moment he asked: 'Where's Mattie?'

Without lifting her eyes from the page she replied: 'I presume she's getting down her trunk.'

The blood rushed to his face. 'Getting down her trunk – alone?'

'Jotham Powell's down in the wood-lot, and Dan'l Byrne says he darsn't leave that horse,' she returned.

Her husband, without stopping to hear the end of the phrase, had left the kitchen and sprung up the stairs. The door of Mattie's room was shut, and he wavered a moment on the landing. 'Matt,' he said in a low voice; but there was no answer, and he put his hand on the doorknob.

He had never been in her room except once, in the early summer, when he had gone there to plaster up a leak in the eaves, but he remembered exactly how everything had looked: the red-and-white quilt on her narrow bed, the pretty pin-cushion on the chest of drawers, and over it the enlarged photograph of her mother, in an oxydised frame, with a bunch of dyed grasses at the back. Now these and all other tokens of her presence had vanished and the room looked as bare and comfortless as when Zeena had shown her into it on the day of her arrival. In the middle of the floor stood her trunk, and on the trunk she sat in her Sunday dress, her back turned to the door and her face in her hands. She had not heard Ethan's call because she was sobbing and she did not hear his step till he stood close behind her and laid his hands on her shoulders.

'Matt – oh, don't – oh, *Matt!*'

She started up, lifting her wet face to his. 'Ethan – I thought I wasn't ever going to see you again!'

He took her in his arms, pressing her close, and with a trembling hand smoothed away the hair from her forehead.

'Not see me again? What do you mean?'

She sobbed out: 'Jotham said you told him we wasn't to wait dinner for you, and I thought – '

'You thought I meant to cut it?' he finished for her grimly.

She clung to him without answering, and he laid his lips on her hair, which was soft yet springy, like certain mosses on warm slopes, and had the faint woody fragrance of fresh sawdust in the sun.

Through the door they heard Zeena's voice calling out from below: 'Dan'l Byrne says you better hurry up if you want him to take that trunk.'

They drew apart with stricken faces. Words of resistance rushed to Ethan's lips and died there. Mattie found her handkerchief and dried her eyes; then, bending down, she took hold of a handle of the trunk.

Ethan put her aside. 'You let go, Matt,' he ordered her.

She answered: 'It takes two to coax it round the corner,' and submitting to this argument he grasped the other handle, and together they manoeuvred the heavy trunk out to the landing.

'Now let go,' he repeated; then he shouldered the trunk and carried it down the stairs and across the passage to the kitchen. Zeena, who had gone back to her seat by the stove, did not lift her head from her book as he passed. Mattie followed him out of the door and helped him to lift the trunk into the back of the sleigh. When it was in place they stood side by side on the doorstep, watching Daniel Byrne plunge off behind his fidgety horse.

It seemed to Ethan that his heart was bound with cords which an unseen hand was tightening with every tick of the clock. Twice he opened his lips to speak to Mattie and found no breath. At length, as she turned to re-enter the house, he laid a detaining hand on her.

'I'm going to drive you over, Matt,' he whispered.

She murmured back: 'I think Zeena wants I should go with Jotham.'

'I'm going to drive you over,' he repeated; and she went into the kitchen without answering.

At dinner Ethan could not eat. If he lifted his eyes they rested on Zeena's pinched face, and the corners of her straight lips seemed to quiver away into a smile. She ate well, declaring that the mild weather made her feel better, and pressed a second helping of beans on Jotham Powell, whose wants she generally ignored.

Mattie, when the meal was over, went about her usual task of clearing the table and washing up the dishes. Zeena, after feeding the cat, had returned to her rocking-chair by the stove, and Jotham

Powell, who always lingered last, reluctantly pushed back his chair and moved toward the door.

On the threshold he turned back to say to Ethan: 'What time'll I come round for Mattie?'

Ethan was standing near the window, mechanically filling his pipe while he watched Mattie move to and fro. He answered: 'You needn't come round; I'm going to drive her over myself.'

He saw the rise of the colour in Mattie's averted cheek, and the quick lifting of Zeena's head.

'I want you should stay here this afternoon, Ethan,' his wife said. 'Jotham can drive Mattie over.'

Mattie flung an imploring glance at him, but he repeated curtly: 'I'm going to drive her over myself.'

Zeena continued in the same even tone: 'I wanted you should stay and fix up that stove in Mattie's room afore the girl gets here. It ain't been drawing right for nigh on a month now.'

Ethan's voice rose indignantly. 'If it was good enough for Mattie I guess it's good enough for a hired girl.'

'That girl that's coming told me she was used to a house where they had a furnace,' Zeena persisted with the same monotonous mildness.

'She'd better ha' stayed there then,' he flung back at her; and turning to Mattie he added in a hard voice: 'You be ready by three, Matt; I've got business at Corbury.'

Jotham Powell had started for the barn, and Ethan strode down after him aflame with anger. The pulses in his temples throbbed and a fog was in his eyes. He went about his task without knowing what force directed him, or whose hands and feet were fulfilling its orders. It was not till he led out the sorrel and backed him between the shafts of the sleigh that he once more became conscious of what he was doing. As he passed the bridle over the horse's head, and wound the traces around the shafts, he remembered the day when he had made the same preparations in order to drive over and meet his wife's cousin at the Flats. It was little more than a year ago, on just such a soft afternoon, with a feel of spring in the air. The sorrel, turning the same big ringed eye on him, nuzzled the palm of his hand in the same way; and one by one all the days between rose up and stood before him . . .

He flung the bearskin into the sleigh, climbed to the seat, and drove up to the house. When he entered the kitchen it was empty, but Mattie's bag and shawl lay ready by the door. He went to the foot of the stairs and listened. No sound reached him from above, but presently he thought he heard someone moving about in his deserted study, and pushing open the door he saw Mattie, in her hat and jacket, standing with her back to him near the table.

She started at his approach and turning quickly, said: 'Is it time?'

'What are you doing here, Matt?' he asked her.

She looked at him timidly. 'I was just taking a look round – that's all,' she answered, with a wavering smile.

They went back into the kitchen without speaking, and Ethan picked up her bag and shawl.

'Where's Zeena?' he asked.

'She went upstairs right after dinner. She said she had those shooting pains again, and didn't want to be disturbed.'

'Didn't she say goodbye to you?'

'No. That was all she said.'

Ethan, looking slowly about the kitchen, said to himself with a shudder that in a few hours he would be returning to it alone. Then the sense of unreality overcame him once more, and he could not bring himself to believe that Mattie stood there for the last time before him.

'Come on,' he said almost gaily, opening the door and putting her bag into the sleigh. He sprang to his seat and bent over to tuck the rug about her as she slipped into the place at his side. 'Now then, go 'long,' he said, with a shake of the reins that sent the sorrel placidly jogging down the hill.

'We got lots of time for a good ride, Matt!' he cried, seeking her hand beneath the fur and pressing it in his. His face tingled and he felt dizzy, as if he had stopped in at the Starkfield saloon on a zero day for a drink.

At the gate, instead of making for Starkfield, he turned the sorrel to the right, up the Bettsbridge road. Mattie sat silent, giving no sign of surprise; but after a moment she said: 'Are you going round by Shadow Pond?'

He laughed and answered: 'I knew you'd know!'

She drew closer under the bearskin, so that, looking sideways around his coat-sleeve, he could just catch the tip of her nose and a blown brown wave of hair. They drove slowly up the road between fields glistening under the pale sun, and then bent to the right down a lane edged with spruce and larch. Ahead of them, a long way off, a range of hills stained by mottlings of black forest flowed away in round white curves against the sky. The lane passed into a pine-wood with boles reddening in the afternoon sun and delicate blue shadows on the snow. As they entered it the breeze fell and a warm stillness seemed to drop from the branches with the dropping needles. Here the snow was so pure that the tiny tracks of wood-animals had left on it intricate lace-like patterns, and the bluish cones caught in its surface stood out like ornaments of bronze.

Ethan drove on in silence till they reached a part of the wood where the pines were more widely spaced, then he drew up and helped Mattie to get out of the sleigh. They passed between the aromatic trunks, the snow breaking crisply under their feet, till they came to a small sheet of water with steep wooded sides. Across its frozen surface, from the farther bank, a single hill rising against the western sun threw the long conical shadow which gave the lake its name. It was a shy secret spot, full of the same dumb melancholy that Ethan felt in his heart.

He looked up and down the little pebbly beach till his eye lit on a fallen tree-trunk half submerged in snow.

'There's where we sat at the picnic,' he reminded her.

The entertainment of which he spoke was one of the few that they had taken part in together: a church picnic which, on a long afternoon of the preceding summer, had filled the retired place with merry-making. Mattie had begged him to go with her but he had refused. Then, toward sunset, coming down from the mountain where he had been felling timber, he had been caught by some strayed revellers and drawn into the group by the lake, where Mattie, encircled by facetious youths, and bright as a blackberry under her spreading hat, was brewing coffee over a gypsy fire. He remembered the shyness he had felt at approaching her in his uncouth clothes, and then the lighting up of her face, and the way she had broken through the group to come to him with a cup in her hand. They had sat for a few minutes on the fallen log by the pond, and she had missed her gold locket, and set the young men searching for it; and it was Ethan who had spied it in the moss . . . That was all; but all their intercourse had been made up of just such inarticulate flashes, when they seemed to come suddenly upon happiness as if they had surprised a butterfly in the winter woods . . .

'It was right there I found your locket,' he said, pushing his foot into a dense tuft of blueberry bushes.

'I never saw anybody with such sharp eyes!' she answered.

She sat down on the tree-trunk in the sun and he sat down beside her.

'You were as pretty as a picture in that pink hat,' he said.

She laughed with pleasure. 'Oh, I guess it was the hat!' she rejoined.

They had never before avowed their inclination so openly, and

Ethan, for a moment, had the illusion that he was a free man, wooing the girl he meant to marry. He looked at her hair and longed to touch it again, and to tell her that it smelt of the woods; but he had never learned to say such things.

Suddenly she rose to her feet and said: 'We mustn't stay here any longer.'

He continued to gaze at her vaguely, only half-roused from his dream. 'There's plenty of time,' he answered.

They stood looking at each other as if the eyes of each were straining to absorb and hold fast the other's image. There were things he had to say to her before they parted, but he could not say them in that place of summer memories, and he turned and followed her in silence to the sleigh. As they drove away the sun sank behind the hill and the pine-boles turned from red to grey.

By a devious track between the fields they wound back to the Starkfield road. Under the open sky the light was still clear, with a reflection of cold red on the eastern hills. The clumps of trees in the snow seemed to draw together in ruffled lumps, like birds with their heads under their wings; and the sky, as it paled, rose higher, leaving the earth more alone.

As they turned into the Starkfield road Ethan said: 'Matt, what do you mean to do?'

She did not answer at once, but at length she said: 'I'll try to get a place in a store.'

'You know you can't do it. The bad air and the standing all day nearly killed you before.'

'I'm a lot stronger than I was before I came to Starkfield.'

'And now you're going to throw away all the good it's done you!'

There seemed to be no answer to this, and again they drove on for a while without speaking. With every yard of the way some spot where they had stood, and laughed together or been silent, clutched at Ethan and dragged him back.

'Isn't there any of your father's folks could help you?'

'There isn't any of 'em I'd ask.'

He lowered his voice to say: 'You know there's nothing I wouldn't do for you if I could.'

'I know there isn't.'

'But I can't – '

She was silent, but he felt a slight tremor in the shoulder against his.

'Oh, Matt,' he broke out, 'if I could ha' gone with you now I'd ha' done it – '

She turned to him, pulling a scrap of paper from her breast. 'Ethan – I found this,' she stammered. Even in the failing light he saw it was the letter to his wife that he had begun the night before and forgotten to destroy. Through his astonishment there ran a fierce thrill of joy. 'Matt – ' he cried; 'if I could ha' done it, would you?'

'Oh, Ethan, Ethan – what's the use?' With a sudden movement she tore the letter in shreds and sent them fluttering off into the snow.

'Tell me, Matt! Tell me!' he adjured her.

She was silent for a moment; then she said, in such a low tone that he had to stoop his head to hear her: 'I used to think of it sometimes, summer nights, when the moon was so bright I couldn't sleep.'

His heart reeled with the sweetness of it. 'As long ago as that?'

She answered, as if the date had long been fixed for her: 'The first time was at Shadow Pond.'

'Was that why you gave me my coffee before the others?'

'I don't know. Did I? I was dreadfully put out when you wouldn't go to the picnic with me; and then, when I saw you coming down the road, I thought maybe you'd gone home that way o' purpose; and that made me glad.'

They were silent again. They had reached the point where the road dipped to the hollow by Ethan's mill and as they descended the darkness descended with them, dropping down like a black veil from the heavy hemlock boughs.

'I'm tied hand and foot, Matt. There isn't a thing I can do,' he began again.

'You must write to me sometimes, Ethan.'

'Oh, what good'll writing do? I want to put my hand out and touch you. I want to do for you and care for you. I want to be there when you're sick and when you're lonesome.'

'You mustn't think but what I'll do all right.'

'You won't need me, you mean? I suppose you'll marry!'

'Oh, Ethan!' she cried.

'I don't know how it is you make me feel, Matt. I'd a'most rather have you dead than that!'

'Oh, I wish I was, I wish I was!' she sobbed.

The sound of her weeping shook him out of his dark anger, and he felt ashamed.

'Don't let's talk that way,' he whispered.

'Why shouldn't we, when it's true? I've been wishing it every minute of the day.'

'Matt! You be quiet! Don't you say it.'

'There's never anybody been good to me but you.'

'Don't say that either, when I can't lift a hand for you!'

'Yes; but it's true just the same.'

They had reached the top of School House Hill and Starkfield lay below them in the twilight. A cutter, mounting the road from the village, passed them by in a joyous flutter of bells, and they straightened themselves and looked ahead with rigid faces. Along the main street lights had begun to shine from the house-fronts and stray figures were turning in here and there at the gates. Ethan, with a touch of his whip, roused the sorrel to a languid trot.

As they drew near the end of the village the cries of children reached them, and they saw a knot of boys, with sleds behind them, scattering across the open space before the church.

'I guess this'll be their last coast for a day or two,' Ethan said, looking up at the mild sky. Mattie was silent, and he added: 'We were to have gone down last night.' Still she did not speak and, prompted by an obscure desire to help himself and her through their miserable last hour, he went on discursively: 'Ain't it funny we haven't been down together but just that once last winter?'

She answered: 'It wasn't often I got down to the village.'

'That's so,' he said.

They had reached the crest of the Corbury road, and between the indistinct white glimmer of the church and the black curtain of the Varnum spruces the slope stretched away below them without a sled on its length. Some erratic impulse prompted Ethan to say: 'How'd you like me to take you down now?'

She forced a laugh. 'Why, there isn't time!'

'There's all the time we want. Come along!' His one desire now was to postpone the moment of turning the sorrel toward the Flats.

'But the girl,' she faltered. 'The girl'll be waiting at the station.'

'Well, let her wait. You'd have to if she didn't. Come!'

The note of authority in his voice seemed to subdue her, and when he had jumped from the sleigh she let him help her out, saying only, with a vague feint of reluctance: 'But there isn't a sled round anywheres.'

'Yes, there is! Right over there under the spruces.'

He threw the bearskin over the sorrel, who stood passively by the roadside, hanging a meditative head. Then he caught Mattie's hand and drew her after him toward the sled.

She seated herself obediently and he took his place behind her, so close that her hair brushed his face. 'All right, Matt?' he called out, as if the width of the road had been between them.

She turned her head to say: 'It's dreadfully dark. Are you sure you can see?'

He laughed contemptuously: 'I could go down this coast with my eyes tied!' and she laughed with him, as if she liked his audacity. Nevertheless he sat still a moment, straining his eyes down the long hill, for it was the most confusing hour of the evening, the hour when the last clearness from the upper sky is merged with the rising night in a blur that disguises landmarks and falsifies distances.

'Now!' he cried.

The sled started with a bound, and they flew on through the dusk, gathering smoothness and speed as they went, with the hollow night opening out below them and the air singing by like an organ. Mattie sat perfectly still, but as they reached the bend at the foot of the hill, where the big elm thrust out a deadly elbow, he fancied that she shrank a little closer.

'Don't be scared, Matt!' he cried exultantly, as they spun safely past it and flew down the second slope; and when they reached the level ground beyond, and the speed of the sled began to slacken, he heard her give a little laugh of glee.

They sprang off and started to walk back up the hill. Ethan dragged the sled with one hand and passed the other through Mattie's arm.

'Were you scared I'd run you into the elm?' he asked with a boyish laugh.

'I told you I was never scared with you,' she answered.

The strange exaltation of his mood had brought on one of his rare fits of boastfulness. 'It *is* a tricky place, though. The least swerve, and we'd never ha' come up again. But I can measure distances to a hair's-breadth – always could.'

She murmured: 'I always say you've got the surest eye . . . '

Deep silence had fallen with the starless dusk, and they leaned on each other without speaking; but at every step of their climb Ethan said to himself: 'It's the last time we'll ever walk together.'

They mounted slowly to the top of the hill. When they were abreast of the church he stooped his head to her to ask: 'Are you tired?' and she answered, breathing quickly: 'It was splendid!'

With a pressure of his arm he guided her toward the Norway spruces. 'I guess this sled must be Ned Hale's. Anyhow I'll leave it where I found it.' He drew the sled up to the Varnum gate and rested it against the fence. As he raised himself he suddenly felt Mattie close to him among the shadows.

'Is this where Ned and Ruth kissed each other?' she whispered breathlessly, and flung her arms about him. Her lips, groping for his, swept over his face, and he held her fast in a rapture of surprise.

'Goodbye – goodbye,' she stammered, and kissed him again.

'Oh, Matt, I can't let you go!' broke from him in the same old cry.

She freed herself from his hold and he heard her sobbing. 'Oh, I can't go either!' she wailed.

'Matt! What'll we do? What'll we do?'

They clung to each other's hands like children, and her body shook with desperate sobs.

Through the stillness they heard the church clock striking five.

'Oh, Ethan, it's time!' she cried.

He drew her back to him. 'Time for what? You don't suppose I'm going to leave you now?'

'If I missed my train where'd I go?'

'Where are you going if you catch it?'

She stood silent, her hands lying cold and relaxed in his.

'What's the good of either of us going anywheres without the other one now?' he said.

She remained motionless, as if she had not heard him. Then she snatched her hands from his, threw her arms about his neck, and pressed a sudden drenched cheek against his face. 'Ethan! Ethan! I want you to take me down again!'

'Down where?'

'The coast. Right off,' she panted. 'So 't we'll never come up any more.'

'Matt! What on earth do you mean?'

She put her lips close against his ear to say: 'Right into the big elm. You said you could. So 't we'd never have to leave each other any more.'

'Why, what are you talking of? You're crazy!'

'I'm not crazy; but I will be if I leave you.'

'Oh, Matt, Matt – ' he groaned.

She tightened her fierce hold about his neck. Her face lay close to his face.

'Ethan, where'll I go if I leave you? I don't know how to get along alone. You said so yourself just now. Nobody but you was ever good to me. And there'll be that strange girl in the house . . . and she'll sleep in my bed, where I used to lay nights and listen to hear you come up the stairs . . . '

The words were like fragments torn from his heart. With them came the hated vision of the house he was going back to – of the stairs he would have to go up every night, of the woman who would wait for him there. And the sweetness of Mattie's avowal, the wild wonder of knowing at last that all that had happened to him had happened to her too, made the other vision more abhorrent, the other life more intolerable to return to . . .

Her pleadings still came to him between short sobs, but he no longer heard what she was saying. Her hat had slipped back and he was stroking her hair. He wanted to get the feeling of it into his hand, so that it would sleep there like a seed in winter. Once he found her mouth again, and they seemed to be by the pond together in the burning August sun. But his cheek touched hers, and it was cold and full of weeping, and he saw the road to the Flats under the night and heard the whistle of the train up the line.

The spruces swathed them in blackness and silence. They might have been in their coffins underground. He said to himself: 'Perhaps it'll feel like this . . .' and then again: 'After this I shan't feel anything . . . ' Suddenly he heard the old sorrel whinny across the road, and thought: 'He's wondering why he doesn't get his supper . . . '

'Come,' Mattie whispered, tugging at his hand.

Her sombre violence constrained him: she seemed the embodied instrument of fate. He pulled the sled out, blinking like a night-bird as he passed from the shade of the spruces into the trans parent dusk of the open. The slope below them was deserted. All Starkfield was at supper, and not a figure crossed the open space before the church. The sky, swollen with the clouds that announce a thaw, hung as low as before a summer storm. He strained his eyes through the dimness, and they seemed less keen, less capable than usual.

He took his seat on the sled and Mattie instantly placed herself in front of him. Her hat had fallen into the snow and his lips were in her hair. He stretched out his legs, drove his heels into the road to keep the sled from slipping forward, and bent her head back between his hands. Then suddenly he sprang up again.

'Get up,' he ordered her.

It was the tone she always heeded, but she cowered down in her seat, repeating, vehemently: 'No, no, no!'

'Get up!'

'Why?'

'I want to sit in front.'

'No, no! How can you steer in front?'

'I don't have to. We'll follow the track.'

They spoke in smothered whispers, as though the night were listening.

'Get up! Get up!' he urged her; but she kept on repeating: 'Why do you want to sit in front?'

'Because I – because I want to feel you holding me,' he stammered, and dragged her to her feet.

The answer seemed to satisfy her, or else she yielded to the power of his voice. He bent down, feeling in the obscurity for the glassy slide worn by preceding coasters, and placed the runners carefully between its edges. She waited while he seated himself with crossed legs in the front of the sled; then she crouched quickly down at his back and clasped her arms about him. Her breath on his neck set him shuddering again, and he almost sprang from his seat. But in a flash he remembered the alternative. She was right: this was better than parting. He leaned back and drew her mouth to his . . .

Just as they started he heard the sorrel's whinny again, and the familiar wistful call, and all the confused images it brought with it, went with him down the first reach of the road. Half-way down there was a sudden drop, then a rise, and after that another long delirious descent. As they took wing for this it seemed to him that they were flying indeed, flying far up into the cloudy night, with Starkfield immeasurably below them, falling away like a speck in space . . . Then the big elm shot up ahead, lying in wait for them at the bend of the road, and he said between his teeth: 'We can fetch it; I know we can fetch it – '

As they flew toward the tree Mattie pressed her arms tighter, and her blood seemed to be in his veins. Once or twice the sled swerved a little under them. He slanted his body to keep it headed for the elm, repeating to himself again and again: 'I know we can fetch it'; and little phrases she had spoken ran through his head and danced before him on the air. The big tree loomed bigger and closer, and as they bore down on it he thought: 'It's waiting for us: it seems to know.' But suddenly his wife's face, with twisted monstrous lineaments, thrust itself between him and his goal, and he made an instinctive movement to brush it aside. The sled swerved in response, but he righted it again, kept it straight, and drove down on the black projecting mass. There was a last instant when the air shot past him like millions of fiery wires; and then the elm . . .

The sky was still thick, but looking straight up he saw a single star, and tried vaguely to reckon whether it were Sirius,[30] or – or – The effort tired him too much, and he closed his heavy lids and thought that he would sleep . . . The stillness was so profound that he heard a little animal twittering somewhere nearby under the snow. It made a small frightened *cheep* like a field mouse, and he wondered languidly

if it were hurt. Then he understood that it must be in pain: pain so
excruciating that he seemed, mysteriously, to feel it shooting
through his own body. He tried in vain to roll over in the direction of
the sound, and stretched his left arm out across the snow. And now it
was as though he felt rather than heard the twittering; it seemed to
be under his palm, which rested on something soft and springy. The
thought of the animal's suffering was intolerable to him and he
struggled to raise himself, and could not because a rock, or some
huge mass, seemed to be lying on him. But he continued to finger
about cautiously with his left hand, thinking he might get hold of the
little creature and help it; and all at once he knew that the soft thing
he had touched was Mattie's hair and that his hand was on her face.

He dragged himself to his knees, the monstrous load on him
moving with him as he moved, and his hand went over and over her
face, and he felt that the twittering came from her lips . . .

He got his face down close to hers, with his ear to her mouth, and
in the darkness he saw her eyes open and heard her say his name.

'Oh, Matt, I thought we'd fetched it,' he moaned; and far off, up
the hill, he heard the sorrel whinny, and thought: 'I ought to be
getting him his feed . . . ' . . . .
. . . .
. . . .
. . . .

CHAPTER TEN

THE QUERULOUS DRONE ceased as I entered Frome's kitchen, and of the two women sitting there I could not tell which had been the speaker.

One of them, on my appearing, raised her tall bony figure from her seat, not as if to welcome me – for she threw me no more than a brief glance of surprise – but simply to set about preparing the meal which Frome's absence had delayed. A slatternly calico wrapper hung from her shoulders and the wisps of her thin grey hair were drawn away from a high forehead and fastened at the back by a broken comb. She had pale opaque eyes which revealed nothing and reflected nothing, and her narrow lips were of the same sallow colour as her face.

The other woman was much smaller and slighter. She sat huddled in an armchair near the stove, and when I came in she turned her head quickly toward me, without the least corresponding movements of her body. Her hair was as grey as her companion's, her face as bloodless and shrivelled, but amber-tinted, with swarthy shadows sharpening the nose and hollowing the temples. Under her shapeless dress her body kept its limp immobility, and her dark eyes had the bright witch-like stare that disease of the spine sometimes gives.

Even for that part of the country the kitchen was a poor-looking place. With the exception of the dark-eyed woman's chair, which looked like a soiled relic of luxury bought at a country auction, the furniture was of the roughest kind. Three coarse china plates and a broken-nosed milk-jug had been set on a greasy table scored with knife-cuts, and a couple of straw-bottomed chairs and a kitchen dresser of unpainted pine stood meagrely against the plaster walls.

'My, it's cold here! The fire must be 'most out,' Frome said, glancing about him apologetically as he followed me in.

The tall woman, who had moved away from us toward the dresser, took no notice; but the other, from her cushioned niche, answered complainingly, in a high thin voice. 'It's on'y just been made up this very minute. Zeena fell asleep and slep' ever so long, and I thought I'd be frozen stiff before I could wake her up and get her to 'tend to it.'

I knew then that it was she who had been speaking when we entered.

Her companion, who was just coming back to the table with the remains of a cold mince-pie in a battered pie-dish, set down her unappetising burden without appearing to hear the accusation brought against her.

Frome stood hesitatingly before her as she advanced; then he looked at me and said: 'This is my wife, Mis' Frome.' After another interval he added, turning toward the figure in the armchair: 'And this is Miss Mattie Silver . . . '

. . . .

Mrs Hale, tender soul, had pictured me as lost in the Flats and buried under a snowdrift; and so lively was her satisfaction on seeing me safely restored to her the next morning that I felt my peril had caused me to advance several degrees in her favour.

Great was her amazement, and that of old Mrs Varnum, on learning that Ethan Frome's old horse had carried me to and from Corbury Junction through the worst blizzard of the winter; greater still their surprise when they heard that his master had taken me in for the night.

Beneath their wondering exclamations I felt a secret curiosity to know what impressions I had received from my night in the Frome household, and divined that the best way of breaking down their reserve was to let them try to penetrate mine. I therefore confined myself to saying, in a matter-of-fact tone, that I had been received with great kindness, and that Frome had made a bed for me in a room on the ground floor which seemed in happier days to have been fitted up as a kind of writing-room or study.

'Well,' Mrs Hale mused, 'in such a storm I suppose he felt he couldn't do less than take you in – but I guess it went hard with Ethan. I don't believe but what you're the only stranger has set foot in that house for over twenty years. He's that proud he don't even like his oldest friends to go there; and I don't know as any do, any more, except myself and the doctor . . . '

'You still go there, Mrs Hale?' I ventured.

'I used to go a good deal after the accident, when I was first married; but after a while I got to think it made 'em feel worse to see us. And then one thing and another came, and my own troubles . . . But I generally make out to drive over there round about New Year's, and once in the summer. Only I always try to pick a day when Ethan's off somewhere. It's bad enough to see the two women sitting there – but *his* face, when he looks round that bare place, just kills me . . . You see, I can look back and call it up in his mother's day, before their troubles.'

Old Mrs Varnum, by this time, had gone up to bed, and her daughter and I were sitting alone, after supper, in the austere seclusion of the horsehair parlour. Mrs Hale glanced at me tentatively, as though trying to see how much footing my conjectures gave her; and I guessed that if she had kept silence till now it was because she had been waiting, through all the years, for someone who should see what she alone had seen.

I waited to let her trust in me gather strength before I said: 'Yes, it's pretty bad, seeing all three of them there together.'

She drew her mild brows into a frown of pain. 'It was just awful from the beginning. I was here in the house when they were carried up – they laid Mattie Silver in the room you're in. She and I were great friends, and she was to have been my bridesmaid in the spring . . . When she came to I went up to her and stayed all night. They gave her things to quiet her, and she didn't know much till to'rd morning, and then all of a sudden she woke up just like herself, and looked straight at me out of her big eyes, and said . . . Oh, I don't know why I'm telling you all this,' Mrs Hale broke off, crying.

She took off her spectacles, wiped the moisture from them, and put them on again with an unsteady hand. 'It got about the next day,' she went on, 'that Zeena Frome had sent Mattie off in a hurry because she had a hired girl coming, and the folks here could never rightly tell what she and Ethan were doing that night coasting, when they'd ought to have been on their way to the Flats to ketch the train . . . I never knew myself what Zeena thought – I don't to this day. Nobody knows Zeena's thoughts. Anyhow, when she heard o' the accident she came right in and stayed with Ethan over to the minister's, where they'd carried him. And as soon as the doctors said that Mattie could be moved, Zeena sent for her and took her back to the farm.'

'And there she's been ever since?'

Mrs Hale answered simply: 'There was nowhere else for her to go'; and my heart tightened at the thought of the hard compulsions of the poor.

'Yes, there she's been,' Mrs Hale continued, 'and Zeena's done for her, and done for Ethan, as good as she could. It was a miracle, considering how sick she was – but she seemed to be raised right up just when the call came to her. Not as she's ever given up doctoring, and she's had sick spells right along; but she's had the strength given her to care for those two for over twenty years, and before the accident came she thought she couldn't even care for herself.'

Mrs Hale paused a moment, and I remained silent, plunged in the vision of what her words evoked. 'It's horrible for them all,' I murmured.

'Yes, it's pretty bad. And they ain't any of 'em easy people either. Mattie *was*, before the accident; I never knew a sweeter nature. But she's suffered too much – that's what I always say when folks tell me how she's soured. And Zeena, she was always cranky. Not but what she bears with Mattie wonderful – I've seen that myself. But sometimes the two of them get going at each other, and then Ethan's face'd break your heart . . . When I see that, I think it's *him* that suffers most . . . anyhow, it ain't Zeena, because she ain't got the time . . . It's a pity, though,' Mrs Hale ended, sighing, 'that they're all shut up there 'n that one kitchen. In the summertime, on pleasant days, they move Mattie into the parlour, or out in the door-yard, and that makes it easier . . . but winters there's the fires to be thought of; and there ain't a dime to spare up at the Fromes'.'

Mrs Hale drew a deep breath, as though her memory were eased of its long burden, and she had no more to say; but suddenly an impulse of complete avowal seized her.

She took off her spectacles again, leaned toward me across the bead-work table-cover, and went on with lowered voice: 'There was one day, about a week after the accident, when they all thought Mattie couldn't live. Well, I say it's a pity she *did*. I said it right out to our minister once, and he was shocked at me. Only he wasn't with me that morning when she first came to . . . And I say, if she'd ha' died, Ethan might ha' lived; and the way they are now, I don't see's there's much difference between the Fromes up at the farm and the Fromes down in the graveyard; 'cept that down there they're all quiet, and the women have got to hold their tongues.'

NOTES

1 (p. 29) *my imaginary Starkfield*   Edith Wharton located her village in the region around Lenox in the Berkshire Hills, Western Massachusetts, where she owned The Mount, her summer estate from 1902–11.

2 (p. 29) *New England of fiction*   specifically identified by Wharton elsewhere as the stories of Local Colour writers such as Sarah Orne Jewett (1849–1909) and Mary E. Wilkins Freeman (1852–1930)

3 (p. 31) *La Grande Bretêche*   [Bretèche] by Honoré de Balzac (1799–1850), a short story (1832) in which the narrator tries to penetrate the mystery of a dilapidated old house and its once-beautiful garden

4 (p. 31) *The Ring and the Book*   by Robert Browning (1812–1889), a dramatic poem (1868–9) about a Roman murder case of 1698, presented through the different perspectives of twelve narrators

5 (p. 33) *pre-trolley days*   the era of horse-drawn transport, before the arrival of the electric tram-car. Running on lines and powered by overhead cables, trolleys became a feature of many New England towns after the turn of the century (lines were laid at Lenox in 1901–02).

6 (p. 34) *his specific*   a treatment aimed at a particular symptom, ailment or part of the body

7 (p. 35) *rural delivery*   free delivery of mail direct to country homes, instituted in 1898

8 (p. 35) *YMCA halls*   facilities for the Young Men's Christian Association, a non-profit-making community organisation aimed at improving 'the spiritual, mental, social and physical conditions of young men' (1866). Founded in London in 1844 and in Boston in 1851, the YMCA rapidly established itself in the United States, and was noted for its affordable lodgings and good recreational amenities.

9 (p. 35) *the big power-house*   for generating and distributing electricity

10 (p. 36) *Carcel lamp*   Also called 'French' or 'mechanical' lamp
    and invented by Frenchman B. G. Carcel (1750–1812), oil was
    pumped up its wick by clockwork.

11 (p. 43) *the Dipper . . . Orion*   constellations in the northern part
    of the sky, seen most clearly over the winter months. The 'Big
    Dipper' (the US name for the Plough) and the 'Little Dipper'
    (*Ursa Minor* or the Little Bear) are both said to be shaped like a
    ladle; 'Orion', the largest of all the groups of stars, is named after
    the great hunter of Greek legend, who was held to have been
    transformed into a constellation after his death.

12 (p. 43) *an exhausted receiver*   technical apparatus used in physics:
    a large glass bell jar, from which air had been pumped out to
    create a vacuum

13 (p. 43) *Worcester*   the second city of Massachusetts, known as the
    'heart of the commonwealth', with 84,655 inhabitants by 1890

14 (p. 44) *'fascinator'*   a woman's head-covering, made of lace or
    crochet, so-called because it half revealed, half concealed

15 (p. 46) *Aldebaran*   a conspicuous reddish star, the brightest in
    the constellation of the Bull (*Taurus*)

16 (p. 46) *the Pleiades*   a beautiful group of stars, only half a dozen
    of which are visible to the naked eye; also known as the 'Seven
    Sisters' or the 'Hen and Chickens'

17 (p. 48) *turnip-watch*   a thick, large old-fashioned watch

18 (p. 55) *crimping-pins*   narrow metal grips for waving the hair

19 (p. 58) *indentured*   secured by binding contract, to serve with
    little or no pay

20 (p. 58) *'Curfew shall not ring tonight'*   a poem by Rose Hartwick
    Thorpe (1850–1939), about Bessie who risks her life to save Basil,
    her lover, condemned to die at twilight. It was a favourite ballad
    for parlour recitation, and was further popularised in a number of
    versions set to music (e.g 'Hang on the bell, Nellie').

21 (p. 58) *'The Lost Chord'*   (1877) hugely popular religious song for
    piano accompaniment, from the poem by Adelaide Anne Proctor
    (1825–64), music by Arthur Sullivan (1842–1900). It had sold
    over half a million copies in the United States by the end of the
    century (its fame further promoted by the story that Sullivan had
    composed it by his dying brother's bedside).

22 (p. 58) *a pot-pourri from 'Carmen'* a medley from the opera by Georges Bizet (1838–75), from the novel by Prosper Mérimée (1803–70), the story of an alluring Spanish gypsy girl

23 (p. 59) *Springfield* an industrial city in Western Masachusetts, with 44,179 inhabitants by 1890

24 (p. 59) *an electric battery* a patent device exploiting popular belief in the restorative powers of electricity, one of many variants (e.g. the electric belt, the electric corset, the galvanic bath) mass-marketed for decades after Edison's first commercial ventures in the late 1870s

25 (p. 65) *'cupolo'* (cupola), a small decorative dome on a roof

26 (p. 77) *traveller's joy* the wild clematis, a flowering vine with clinging tendrils

27 (p. 80) *'nervous'* an all-purpose term for a range of physical and psychological conditions, from being 'highly strung' to being in a state of severe mental or emotional disturbance; here, exhausted, tense and agitated

28 (p. 91) *Abraham Lincoln* revered leader (1809–65), sixteenth president of the USA, 1860–5

29 (p. 95) *huckabuck towel* towel made of rough linen or cotton

30 (p. 109) *Sirius* the Dog Star, a brilliant blue-white, the brightest fixed star in the whole of our skies